THE EMPTY ROOM

Books by Charles Morgan

———

MY NAME IS LEGION (1925)

PORTRAIT IN A MIRROR (1929)

THE FOUNTAIN (1932)

SPARKENBROKE (1936)

THE VOYAGE (1940)

———

EPITAPH ON GEORGE MOORE (1935)

THE FLASHING STREAM (1938)
(A Play, with an Essay on Singleness of Mind)

THE
EMPTY ROOM

BY

CHARLES MORGAN

" Why rushed the discords in, but that harmony should be prized ? . . .
I will be patient and proud, and soberly acquiesce.
Give me the keys. I feel for the common chord again,
Sliding by semitones, till I sink to the minor. . . . "

ROBERT BROWNING

LONDON
MACMILLAN & CO. LTD
1941

PRINTED IN GREAT BRITAIN
BY R. & R. CLARK, LIMITED, EDINBURGH

CONTENTS

PAGE

PART ONE I

> "I have been young and now am not too old;
> And I have seen the righteous forsaken,
> His health, his honour and his quality taken.
> This is not what we were formerly told."

PART TWO 49

> "I knew Seraphina; Nature gave her hue,
> Glance, sympathy, note, like one from Eden.
> I saw her smile warp, heard her lyric deaden;
> She turned to harlotry; — this I took to be new."

PART THREE 97

> "Say what you will, our God sees how they run.
> These disillusions are His curious proving
> That He loves humanity and will go on loving;
> Over there are faith, life, virtue in the sun."

The verses above are from Edmund Blunden's *Report on Experience* and are reprinted here by his generous permission.

PART ONE

"I have been young and now am not too old ;
  And I have seen the righteous forsaken,
    His health, his honour and his quality taken.
    This is not what we were formerly told."

EDMUND BLUNDEN

PART ONE

O N the last Saturday in November, the third month of the war, Richard Cannock performed, on a woman's eye, a bold and subtle operation that gave him the satisfaction a writer may have in a flawless paragraph. He went in for luncheon to the Garrick Club and seated himself at the long table. On his left was an actor of seniority and distinction to whom, as to most others, the stage was now closed ; on his right, Copley Deedes, a surgeon younger than himself by three or four years, young enough to have missed the last war.

Silent by habit, Cannock, after a nod to each of them, ordered his meal and looked round the room. The best pictures were gone " to a place of safety," only their empty frames hung on the walls, and he thought : there's a compensating adventure in an empty frame — you can imagine a masterpiece for yourself ; but he regretted the Zoffanys, and particularly the one that had always hung over the fireplace, the most beautiful Zoffany in the world.

He spoke to the actor of this, for he could not speak of the theatre, which both loved and was dead. The wine-steward brought his pint of claret. Then, suddenly, speaking out of his private thought but with an abrupt turn of the head towards Copley Deedes, Cannock said : " I operated this morning."

It wasn't particularly to be commented upon that Cannock, as eminent an ophthalmic surgeon as any in London, had operated this morning, and Deedes, looking up, permitted himself a deliberate Americanism : " And so, what ? "

Cannock, having spoken less to Deedes than to himself, drew away from the question, but was bound to answer it.

" Probably the last," he said, " anyhow for a long time."

" The last what ? "

" Operation."

A note of sympathy was introduced into Deedes's voice. Perhaps he thought that Cannock's own sight was failing. " Nothing wrong ? " he said, and Cannock, wishing to heaven that he had not begun this conversation which was leading or might lead to a kind of theatricalism that he abhorred, answered : " Oh no, nothing. A war job, that's all. I brought it on myself. It will take me out of practice for the duration " — and before Deedes could ask the inevitable questions he shied away from the subject.

Almost with violence he caught at the old actor's conversation, which was sounding in his left ear, about his palmy days with George Alexander at the St. James's Theatre and about the film director who, last Thursday, had told him, who had indeed presumed to *show* him, how to take snuff : " Lord bless me soul, the little chap did it with a flourish he must have learned beside a barber's chair ! "

On Sunday morning Cannock drove himself out of London in his own small car piled with luggage. He had saved petrol for that solitary sixty miles. Glazeden is a bleak railway junction at best, bleaker in war, on Sunday mornings bleakest. A few patient women with empty beer-jugs in their hands were waiting in the rain for the public-houses to open. He drove across the town to the works of Anstey, Rush and Krantree on its northern outskirts. The initials A.R.K., which are a hall-mark throughout the world on range-finders, telescopes, theodolites and scientific instruments of every sort, stood boldly, in wrought-iron monogram, on the gates. Cannock set the bell clanging. While the gates were being opened and the sentry was examining his pass, he stared at the wide courtyard. Duck-boards stretched across its muddy gravel from the small square Lodge, where, he presumed, Research Unit Seven had their living quarters, to the works themselves, a pile of yellow and violet brick sprinkled with those clock-towers, weather-vanes, minarets and pepper-pots that were the architectural dream of manufacturers fifty years ago.

At the door of the Lodge, having rung the bell, he would gladly have escaped. He was so profoundly and intuitively a man of science that he had not the protective skin that others grow when they become important. That he might be welcomed as one who stood near the head of his profession gave him no kind of reassurance. He was going among a group of strangers as he had done when a new boy at school, as he had done again as a subaltern of the Coldstream in the last war, and he did not assume that they would like him. He compelled himself to go in when the door opened and, in the ante-room, to say to the men he found there what he greatly disliked saying : that he was Richard Cannock. They gave him sherry and afterwards food in their mess — he thought of it still as their mess, not his own. He learned that most of them had billets either in Glazeden itself or in the neighbouring villages of West Sarley, Sarley Down and Findon St. Utolph. As no billet had yet been found for him, he was shown a room in the Lodge itself with two beds, a white-painted chest of drawers, a table of packing-cases and an electric light, the bulb dimmed with black paint, hung from mid-ceiling. About the room were scattered the clothes of the electrical engineer from Manchester with whom he would share it.

Chard, the Commander who had made himself his guide, stood at the open door. " I'll leave you. You'll want time to shake down."

" No," Cannock answered quickly. " I'd rather go over to the Ark while the light lasts and see the place I shall work in. I shall like that."

The naval officer grinned and led the way. They crossed the duck-boards in the fading light. The laboratory that had been assigned to Cannock was piled with cases full of his special equipment. They must be unpacked and their contents sorted.

" That ought to keep me quiet for a bit."

" You aren't going to start now ? "

" If I could get my own assistant over. He came down yesterday. An odd youth — as a craftsman in optical glass among the best in England. Trained in Germany. His name's Flower. They've given him rank as a corporal. You wouldn't forget him if you'd seen him. He has light curly hair that leaps up from his forehead like a barmaid's."

" Corporal Flower," Chard said, " is already a little famous. Nothing on earth would keep a uniform cap on that hair until they'd mown it.

Even now he has managed to keep about four inches of vertical spring. I'll send him over."

On his third evening at Glazeden, Cannock, in his laboratory, had reached, by seven o'clock, that particular state of disorder from which, it seemed, order might suddenly emerge. He looked hopefully at the young man in shirt-sleeves who was cataloguing and arranging on steel shelves the bottles and packets which, with the curiosity of a child at a bran-tub, he drew cautiously from a packing-case labelled, in Cannock's handwriting, " Small Specials."

" How tired are we, Flower ? "

" I'm all right, Mr. Cannock," said the young man without looking up from the nib of his fountain pen. " Heow abeout yew ? "

There are not three words in the language that more certainly point to the district of North London in which the speaker had his origin, and Cannock, having a by-interest in phonetics, remembered with a pang that a revival of Shaw's *Pygmalion* was among the last — perhaps was the last play he had seen in London before the war.

" You a playgoer, Flower ? "

" Used to act a bit meself at school," Flower answered, running exploratory fingers through the ample remains of his pale, high-waving hair. " Not

the leads, you know. Young Gobbo. And Le Beau.
Mostly flickers now, I'm afraid, but sometimes one
is worth seeing, don't you think ? Sylvia Sidney's
my favourite."

"Le Beau ?" Cannock inquired.

"Why ! You remember. A courtier in *As You
Like It.*" Flower stood up and quoted perilously :
" ' Hereafter, in a better world than this, I shall desire
more love and knowledge of you.' Don't know why
I remember that. About the only lines I do remember." He continued his work and added after a
pause, as though, fishing in his pocket, he had been
surprised to find in it but a pair of coins : " In fact,
they are the only ones."

"Good lines at the moment."

"Eh ? . . . Oh, I see. ' Hereafter, in a *better*
world——' I suppose so ; still——"

"Don't tell me you like the war ? "

"Not like, no, of course not. Still, I am doing my
own job. I'm better off than some. Better than you,
Mr. Cannock. This isn't your job now, not reelly, is it ?"

"It's very much my job."

"Well yes — and no. It's not surgery. It's not
Queen Anne Street as you might say. But optical
glass *is* my job. I'd rather do it here under you than
where I was. This is exciting — bomb-sights and
the Paramounts."

" The what ? "

" That's what I call the fighter gunsights," Flower explained, a little doubtful of so much fancy in himself. " I thought of it on the way here. Something of yours put it into my head. You remember I asked why Glazeden was called the Ark — this R.U. 7, I mean. You said the Great and Good thought that covering names were worth having. And you remember the Paramount News-Reel ? It shows a movie-camera snooping about ; then it says : ' The Eyes and Ears of the World.' That's what we are — eyes for night fighters."

Cannock accepted the suggestion. " Good," he answered. " Paramounts. So be it." Then to test his assistant's vanity he asked : " What about the bomb-sights ? Have you invented a name for them ? We'll call them Flowers if you like."

" Why ' flowers ' ? "

" If they come to anything — your immortality."

" Mine ? Oh, *that* kind of Flower ! Good Lord, no, Mr. Cannock. I shouldn't like that ! I shouldn't care for it at all ! " the young man exclaimed in explosive agitation. His face blushed hotly ; the pale hair whitened in contrast above a pink and beady forehead.

" Good," Cannock said, " very good. That is why I chose you from the others."

The eyes grew round and he knew that thus his assistant must have looked when he was given a prize at school.

" Why, Mr. Cannock ? "

" You had the qualifications — and, Flower, you had not vanity."

" No," said Flower, " that's true. That's why I couldn't act. But vanity——"

" Is the devil in a job of this kind. Makes men talk outside. You, by the way," Cannock added, " talking of the job, you said just now : ' This is exciting.' Get that out of your head. Where are they going to billet you ? Glazeden ? Well, once you're outside the Ark, you go through the motions of being bored with this place, bored with the Service too, if you like. Nothing to tell. Flat routine. You can say you wish you were a fighter pilot ; that will please the girls ; but unfortunately your eyesight isn't good enough. Understood ? "

Flower waved an assenting head. " Anyhow you needn't worry about me and girls."

Cannock silently registered this dangerous boast. " For the purposes of feminine curiosity," he continued, " you are in a reserved occupation — optical glass — and, when they ask what you make, what *do* you make ? "

"How would 'binoculars for the War Office' do?"

Flower suggested plausibly ; then added with all the savagery of his mild nature : " Though why I should put on these soldier's togs if all I'm making is innocent binoculars Adolf only knows ! "

He frowned at his uniform cap, perched on a wooden case that he was now about to open. Cannock prevented him. To-morrow the electricians would be upon them. " Check over with me the list of what they have to do. Then we'll pack up for the night. It's near nine. I want food and drink. Can you get food at this hour in your mess ? "

" Oh yes," said Flower, not knowing.

When the lists were checked and the steel cupboards locked, Flower surveyed the still disordered room. " I hate mess," he said, seemingly to himself as he tested the shutter bolts. Then, perhaps because he was tired, he turned on his chief and exclaimed with rare petulance : " How I hate it. These cases. Straw and shavings everywhere. Three still untouched. I hoped we should have been through to-night and able to start to-morrow. But no ! Electricians to-morrow. Then plumbers no doubt. Nothing ready. Improvising, improvising. Different to what we're used to in civil life — all the tools ready to your hand. How would it be, every time you were to operate, if you had to make all your instruments first ? Three months since Adolf went into Poland, and here we are, still improvising."

"I assure you, Flower," Cannock answered, "this is paradise compared with the last war. And yet, you know, it's extraordinarily *like*; that's the devil of it. People wasting the same time and talking much the same nonsense. The same jokes, the same optimism — it's like going to a play by a dramatist who may produce an exciting plot but whose style bores you to death. As yet we aren't half-way through Scene One. . . . Come on. I need a drink. There are the keys. Hand them in when you have locked up."

With a flick of his muffled torch to start him on his way, Cannock found the track of duck-board that would take him to the Lodge. A phrase from a newspaper returned to his mind. A journalist had written of this as a "phony war," and he remembered Chard's dry comment: "Send the chap to sea in a destroyer — or, if that would make him sick, tell him to sit on his stern until the spring." So be it. After a time, Cannock knew, you settled down, even to war. In the bitter winter of Sixteen-Seventeen, the last struggle had seemed endless; it had become for him less an interruption of life than life itself; anyhow, he had ceased to think much about the end of it. But surely, at the beginning of a war, still remembering the time when there was peace, it was natural to look forward hungrily, beyond the bracket, to a time when there might be peace again ? Now, in the dark, paddling on the duck-boards, he saw and accepted an infinite endurance, but he couldn't see the end.

Last time, the deep reserves of Victorian prosperity had held together the wreck of the old world. Now, for good or evil, that was gone ; there would be no going back — in that sense, no reconstruction : something new, perhaps, the past disintegrated. His observation of the fact bore no emotional emphasis ; for the second time his life had been plucked from him, and, whatever his intellect might point to, his personal feeling did not carry him — that night at any rate — beyond the bracket. He had no family ; for many years, since chance had hit him in the face, there had been no woman of any value to his life. He didn't think it likely that he would ever do his own work again. Except his determination — a craftsman's will, not an artist's desire — to produce what young Flower called a Paramount and, perhaps, a bomb-sight to excel the whispered American design, he had nothing in particular to live for — which astonished and a little frightened him, who had always had so much. At the end of the tunnel — what ? It was, he reflected with a smile as his feet struck the paved area in front of the Lodge, a question of the kind they used solemnly to ask of death when he was a medical student, and what troubled him now was not that he didn't know the answer but that his expectation, his hope even, made no spring towards it. It was as if there were no end to the tunnel; anyhow he saw no world in the light of it. Each promise of the enthusiasts, still flourishing the carrot of a new heaven and a new earth, because each resembled so nearly the promises of twenty-five years ago, left him cold, the present struggle seeming to him to be different in its nature from the former one. It appeared at the moment, as he had remarked to young Flower, that a stale dramatist was, with certain variations of plot, repeating himself, but the scene would be transformed, slowly or suddenly the familiar outlines would disappear, and he did not know what would replace them. And yet to permit in his mind a block in the continuity of the human race was irrational; it was, moreover, contrary to the faith by which he had lived; and he was glad to escape from the darkness, to find himself in a lighted passage, to see men passing across its farther end into the ante-room, and to hear their voices.

In the mess-room he had expected to find no one, but Chard was there, tall and long-headed, peeling an apple with what might have been a surgeon's hands. A glass of port was at his elbow. Trained as a regular naval officer, he had retired as a lieutenant, plunged into mathematics and wireless, and worked as a civilian on the research staff of Anstey, Rush and Krantree. The war had brought him up from the Reserve of Officers but had changed his work only in adding to it the duties of liaison between the Admiralty and R.U. 7. Wave-lengths were his game and his link with Cannock. They talked of their work and Cannock related Flower's outburst. Chard rose, walked a few yards to the end of the room, put his glass on the mantelshelf and swung round, his back to the fire, his hands gripped behind him, his head thrown up.

"Do you mind my wandering about while you eat ? . . . In a way it's true. I am doing my own job, so is Flower. But you have been switched over to war purposes. If you don't operate for years, does your hand lose its cunning ? " Cannock didn't answer and Chard went on : " You hate this ? Of course you do. More than last time ? "

"At twenty," Cannock said, " life seems pretty long — not so long at forty-four. And then at any rate I believed in the world to come. I thought I was building it. Now — well no, I don't *disbelieve* in it ; I just don't look forward at all. My fault. There'll be a new world all right, whether I look forward to it or not."

"Probably," Chard replied, "a very new one. Personally I don't like the company of squalling infants, though I am assured by women and revolutionaries that muling and puking is a sign of health. I want my civilization to be at least house-trained. That's why I like the French . . . I came back from France last week. I flew over to make a contact at the Sorbonne. Blankets are what Paris is talking about, and the trouble is more than blankets ; they're not happy about this winter in the Maginot. I made contact with our Naval Liaison and drove on to Chartres. Might be the last time. Raining like hell. Aircraft overhead. In the cathedral, all the stained glass gone. White. Pretty bleak, but you do see the architectural lines. Last time I was in Chartres before the war," he added with a twitch of his cheek, " was on a day when they were taking out the Blue Virgin. And still the Anglo-Saxons didn't believe it. My God, and here we are ! . . . I must tell that story to Rydal. There's a man who still believes in the regeneration of mankind — doesn't like the muling and puking more than we do, but discounts it, bless him. He's in to-night. Come and meet him."

Among the half-dozen in the smoking-room were Oliffe, the weedy and brilliant young engineer who shared Cannock's bedroom, Walter Loose, a designer of aircraft, who sat now on an upright chair, his legs crossed, his hands almost primly folded, alert as a stout robin, and, on the fender, Henry Rydal, with a newspaper across his knees.

Chard touched his shoulder. " Henry, here's a new boy for you."

Rydal lifted his eyes slowly from the print ; then suddenly unwound his great length. " New ? Richard Cannock ? But I *know* this one ! How many years ? — seven, on and off. We had the same cranks — or hadn't we ? "

Richard acknowledged it, grateful for a recognition so casually friendly that it had omitted the formality of shaking hands. The name, Rydal, when Chard had spoken it in the mess-room, had rung no bell in his mind ; the Henry had not suggested itself nor the possibility of his being about to renew here a friendship — or was it an acquaintance ? — which, though not intimate in the sense of its having ever been continuous, he had valued for reasons deeply personal and intuitive, and now valued the more in the retrospect which this encounter had suddenly opened to him. Rydal, four or five years his senior, had come to him first as a patient ; they had discovered a common interest in the theatre, then in the historical aspect of Rydal's own profession, the law ; and so in history itself. Their " crank " — the word was familiar to them both — was that they had loved England in the same way : that is, in the light of her continuing destiny, for the sake of her continuing people ; and had judged policy, foreign or domestic, not by its instant benefits but by its long-term values.

" And what were the cranks, if one may ask ? " Walter Loose put in. " I like to know, in a place like this, what kind of madman lives in the next cell."

" Cannock," Rydal said, " that's your cue."

But Richard had no heart for the old argument. " It may be my cue, but I don't take it."

" I will prompt you," Rydal said at once, not allowing even a glance to question, as yet, the change in his friend. Then, to Walter Loose : " The crank in one word is — afforestation."

" That ? " Loose answered. " That's harmless enough." But, knowing Rydal, he beamed and added : " — if that were all ! "

" It isn't. And, if it were — harmless ! Good heavens ! It isn't so considered by the humble servants of the polling-booths. For years politics has consisted chiefly in its opposite : cutting down the trees — beginning, for choice, with the branch your own country is sitting on. Cannock plainly thinks that this time what's left of the forest is coming up by the roots. May be. But we can replant and wait."

" For what ? " Oliffe put in with challenge.

" For the things to grow, Oliffe. What else ? "

" And meanwhile ? " the young man persisted.

" Wait. Do without. Don't fell oak every twenty years."

" If you think that after this show the people are going to wait and do without——"

" I doubt," Chard said, " whether they'll have much alternative. But they'll think they have."

At this Richard found his tongue. This war was different in nature, different in kind, from the last. Much less was expected from it. The English had learned their lesson, even if the Germans hadn't. " Last time," he said, " we expected the hell of a lot — and quickly. A few hard-bitten men foresaw the blizzard ; they clung to the Army to keep warm ; and others, whom the fortunes of war had taken into the Civil Service, dug in there. But the rest fairly rushed for the open — I for one — and grand it was, not despicable, not even foolish as things were — anyhow a bold illusion that we shared with the Americans : we did really believe in a new heaven and a new earth. *Après la guerre finie.* No one would sing that now."

" And with reason," Rydal said. " This, if you come to think of it, is much nearer to being a religious war than an economic one, and no one expects much for himself out of a religious war. And no one is getting much — or will — out of this war or out of the peace. It just won't be there to get, and, if only some demagogue doesn't promise them rabbits out of an empty hat, this time the people know it. There aren't any rewards from a modern victory for the generation that won it. There aren't any rewards at all except a chance to replant. . . . Are you a grandfather, Oliffe ? "

" A what ? "

" You *are* a grandfather, Oliffe."

" I'm not married."

" But you will be. Oliffe is nothing ; the Oliffes are. You plant the tree ; if your son doesn't cut it down, your grandson will have a bit of shade, and his son will build the Ark in time for the next Flood."

Oliffe grinned. " And another Kipling will write a song about it ! "

" I gather," said Walter Loose with a robin's ferocity, " that you disapprove of Kipling ? "

Oliffe stretched his legs. " Neither approve nor disapprove. I'm not a student of him."

Chard knocked out his pipe. " Then you won't resent my telling you why he was a great man. There were two reasons. First, he saw before the rest of us that undiluted numerical democracy doesn't work. We all know it now — from Cripps to Churchill ; and America is finding out. It leads through chaos to tyranny as it has in Germany — and may in France. . . . The other reason is that he could tell a story."

" And both," said Rydal, " are true of Thucydides."

Chard came out of his chair and swung across the room on his way to his billet. " I'm not sure, Henry, that I much like your parallels with the Peloponnesian War. That story didn't end well."

" End ? Athens didn't end. She came up in the Renaissance."

" A long time to wait."

" May be," said Rydal. " It does take time if you have to start again with little but acorns buried in the earth."

When Chard was gone, he set about the task of persuading Oliffe that he hadn't been snubbed and of putting him at his ease. Richard observed the process with delight. It consisted, on the surface, in knowing what questions Oliffe wanted to answer and in asking them ; more profoundly, in neither despising Oliffe nor patronizing him — in genuinely caring to discover his mind and wishing to learn from it. Rydal had an invincible gentleness which, combined with an intellect unafraid to take risks, enabled him to lift others from their fears. He took away Oliffe's suspicions as he might have helped him out of a coat.

" And now you," he said to Richard when they were left together. Another man would have asked :

Why so silent ? What's the matter with you ? and Richard's mind turned away from the as yet unanswerable questions. They were not asked. "Where's your billet ?" Rydal said. "I'm driving back to Sarley Down. I can drop you on the way."

"I haven't a billet as yet. I have a shake-down here until one has been found."

"Come back with me."

"I have an appointment with electricians at nine-thirty."

"I'll drive you over before that — or Carey will. Bring a razor and a tooth-brush. The rest we can provide."

The pleasure, the sense of relief and reassurance, that Richard had in driving away that night in Rydal's car, was disproportionate to its occasion. His perception of this jolted him into saying almost audibly to himself : "You are letting this get on your nerves." Rydal asked what he had said.

"I didn't speak."

"Then, my friend, you are thinking too loud."

Richard leaned back in the car, glad to be enclosed in it, glad to be driven without knowledge of his direction through that moonless winter's night ; and when they turned in at an open gate and halted in the garage, it cost him an effort to get out and make himself useful in closing the double door.

" You are tired," Rydal said.

" I have had a long day."

" I don't mean that. I have never known work put you on edge."

Richard felt his arm taken. He was guided between shrubberies round the end of the house and across a small lawn enclosed by a wall. As they came to the door of the house, he saw, at the level of his eyes, a dimmed pencilling of light at the edge of a blacked-out window. Rydal used his key and they entered a hall, lighted by an oil-lamp, from which a flight of polished and uncarpeted stairs ran up to a shadowy bend.

Rydal, having put Richard's coat and his own into a closet under the stairs' reverse, called out : " Carey, we have a guest ! " and turned the handle of a door at Richard's side. He touched the lintel in warning. " Mind your head. They were little fellows in those days. I'll lead the way."

He stooped and went in eagerly — so eagerly that there was at first something laughable in his disappointment at finding the room empty. He faltered, looked round, then turned to Richard, whether to explain or to seek reassurance it was hard to tell ; it was a lonely, baffled look, not perfectly covered by his smile.

" Early to bed, I suppose," he said, and added, as though he were speaking of a child : " I'll put my head in on the way upstairs." With that, he dismissed the subject. " We brew tea at this time of night. You see, two cups. Will you share that — or there's some real drink next door ? "

On a wide stone hearth an old fire had been newly made up. Rydal took away a guard that had been propped in front of the embers and set on them a kettle already near to boiling. He crouched in the glow, warming the pot, nursing it in his hands, pouring off the water, putting in tea-leaves to be unfolded by the warmth ; and Richard, watching this calm, domestic ritual, began not so much to observe as to feel the room : its inhabited ease, the pleasant casualness of its old furniture, beautiful, shabby, unmatched ; the carved gleam of portraits — Kneller's, perhaps, or poorer — which, being too large for the walls, added, by the Roman pomp of the men's cloaks or the stiffness of a feminine hand dipped into a basket of flowers, a grace of almost smiling incongruity to the place in which they now found themselves so comfortably at home, as though a great wolf-hound should stretch his length upon a cottage hearth and surprisedly find himself at ease there.

A corner of the room beyond a curtained window-seat on the left of the door was occupied by what

Richard had supposed to be a spinet but was a piano of the early fashion. Above it hung a portrait different from the rest, for, though its subject was a girl in seventeenth-century costume, it had evidently been painted — one would have said by a pupil of Sargent — not more than twenty years ago. Not its style only but the extreme beauty of the sitter made it conspicuous in that room, and Richard, while Henry Rydal was pouring tea into their cups, allowed his eyes to rest upon it.

The girl was very young, perhaps twenty-two or twenty-three years old. She was dark, her eyes wideset, her mouth full-cut, her nose straight and fine, her throat long, delicately carved and of rare strength ; but what lent to the face its special character, communicated by the artist with an authenticity not to be mistaken, was the structure of bone under the eyes, which gave to the cheek a lovely fall and to the eyes themselves a vitality of — of what ? not precisely of alarm, for their expression was tranquil — of wonder, then, of taking nothing for granted, of having heard, amid the timeless delight of being young, an approaching footstep.

Reasonably considered, this expression was natural enough ; youth that is alive has always rumour of the future as age has of the past ; but reason did not lessen the portrait's impact. Richard was penetrated by the foreboding implied in it, as though he were before the likeness of a girl whose fate was already known to him. There appeared in his mind a passage of terror from the most terrible of Horace's Odes, that in which Lydia's old age is hideously prophesied : " *invicem moechos anus arrogantis flebis in solo levis angiportu* . . . thy turn shall come and thou, a forlorn hag in a lonely alley . . ." Against the following lines he shut his memory ; and fear seized him lest this were the portrait of the house's other inhabitant, now sleeping upstairs. Carey ? Rydal's wife ? In the tide of unreason, he saw the sleeping head as the head in the portrait, still young, and shrank from meeting this threatened girl. Then, suddenly, with attempted mockery of his own wild fancy, he remembered that, if this were she, the threat to her youth that he had imagined must long ago have outlived its urgency. By now she must be a woman of above forty years.

Rydal, forcing a cup upon him, drew his gaze from the portrait. The drag of past suffering, that had always underlain the happy composure of his host's face, was now accented. With a kind of entreaty, even with a directive turn of the head like the beckoning gesture of a ghost that cannot speak, Rydal seemed to forbid attention to the picture, and yet he said : " You were looking at that portrait," and Richard answered : " Yes. Who painted it ? " and Rydal, replying with agonized deliberateness to the question that had deliberately not been asked, said : " She was my wife. She died soon afterwards. We were abroad on a holiday after the war, and she died."

Richard wondered whether it would ever become possible for him to say " I was glad that first evening when you told me she had died young," and for Rydal to understand why he said it. Now, seated opposite each other at the fire, they talked of other things. There was a sound of movement in the room above.

" Carey is still up," Rydal said. He was tall enough to reach the low ceiling and hammered on the crossbeam with the side of his fist — a signal evidently understood, for tapping answered it. He returned to the fire smiling, and soon afterwards a girl came in, with step as eager as Rydal's own when he had entered in expectation of finding her ; but, at the turn of the screen masking the door, she halted, with lips parted and swift colour, gathering closer the wrap she wore. She was dressed for the night and had not expected a stranger.

" This is Mr. Cannock," Rydal said. " My daughter, Cannock."

She kissed her father, gave their guest her hand, and seated herself on cushions that Rydal threw down for her on the stone hearth. Firelight reached up to that structure of bone under her eyes which was a seal upon her likeness to her mother — a flawless likeness of age, colour, line, even of expression — and yet, though her youth also heard the approaching footstep and was alive with the knowledge of it, she, unlike the girl in the portrait, heard it with a quiet mind.

She clasped her knees and, with her chin upon them, listened in the attitude of a child, intervening seldom but then with a strange authority, not of opinion but of things seen with her eyes or in her heart. She treated her father sometimes as a sage, sometimes as a gigantic dog whom she loved, and because she seemed to be aware of a link between him and their guest which gave that guest more than courteous privilege, she spoke to Richard with enchanting ease and seriousness, so that he experienced, at the same time, the joy of being welcomed and challenged and laughed with by the very young and the consolation that a man of intellect has so often in the company of one whom he feels to be spiritually wiser than himself.

"I think, Carey," Rydal said when the time had come to light their candles, "that we shall have someone billeted on us before the week is out. Shall you take to it?"

She looked from him to Richard and asked: "You? He means you. Will you come? I should like that."

In the event, more than a week was to pass before Richard transferred his possessions to the Water House and settled there. Each morning, after an early breakfast, he drove himself to Glazeden, returning only at night, sometimes for his evening meal, more often later. His experiments in the Unit began to grip him, but for Flower's sake and because he believed rest to be necessary to good work, he took one day off a week and a week-end in each month.

Though he and his host were thus seldom together for long at a stretch, their friendship had opportunity to deepen, not at the Water House only but at Glazeden also, for though Rydal had no official connexion with the Unit, his qualities made him welcome there, and, as an old friend of Chard's, he had become, since the declaration of war, a frequent visitor to the mess. His private labour to which, since his retirement from active practice at the Bar, he had given himself with increasing devotion, was a survey of legal history from the years preceding 1914 to the present day — a survey particularly directed towards the liberties of the subject and that triangular relationship between citizen, Parliament and Executive which had been so profoundly changed by the earlier war and by the temper of the legislation that had followed it. His purpose was to show, less by argument than by objective history, how far and by what stages the democratic peoples, under the stress of war and the pressure of bureaucracy, had moved away from their principles of freedom ; how, in England, Parliament had delegated to the Executive powers to legislate by decree, how all parties had contributed to this process ; how by a second war it was being expedited. His remedy was the appointment of a Royal Commission charged to review the Laws of England in this light, to weed the whole tangle of emergency legislation, and to indicate by what series of drastic repeals Parliament might, in time of peace, resume the powers it had yielded up. The book he was writing was, primarily, an analysis of the material that such a Commission would have to study. " I am trying to tempt a reforming Lord Chancellor by doing some of his spade-work for him," Rydal would say, but his book amounted to more than that and he knew it : it had application to all the democracies ; it was a pointer to the way in which they might put their own house in order, not by conceding more and more to totalitarian ideas opposed to theirs but by safeguarding their own.

" You see," he said, " the root of the trouble is

this : we have begun to think — and it's an idea common to Nazis and Communists but alien to us and death to us — we have begun to think more and more in terms of an everlasting and all-inclusive State, less and less in terms of the Continuing People for whom the State is nothing more, and should be nothing more, than manager and trustee." He felt that, throughout the world, the humane individualism that is the philosophic root of democracy was being trodden under, but he believed in its vitality and persistent fruitfulness, its power to be reborn, to live again. "But only at a price. Not by shrinking. Not by going slack between wars or pretending that there will never be war again. Certainly not by clamouring for bread and circuses or by telling the Trustees to distribute the trust funds now and let posterity go hang."

The idea of regeneration dominated Rydal's life, and nothing so certainly moved his gentle but abrupt nature to resistance as a denial of it. One afternoon at Glazeden, Flower was rash enough to say that what he called "The System" must be destroyed as a preliminary to the growth of a better society. He and Richard were at work together and Rydal, who had come over to the laboratory to ask whether Richard was ready to drive home, stood at a window looking out on the iron January day.

" 'The System' ? " Rydal demanded, and Flower

came out with the familiar complaint that the world's wealth was unjustly distributed and backed it with the familiar instance : that while men were eager for coffee, coffee had been burnt in Brazil.

" And when that is admitted," said Rydal, " will you tell me that the remedy is to deliver such a blow at the existing system that distribution breaks down altogether and foreign trade stops and each nation withdraws into the shell of a closed economy ? As far as economics are concerned, isn't the plain answer that you can't be a creditor country and a tariff country at the same time ? But it's an answer that takes working out. The world is very sick, Mr. Flower, but you won't cure the patient by kicking him out of bed. And it's not the men of violence only or the greedy men only who have brought him to the state he is in but the impatient humanitarians. Oh, I know," he added when Flower would have spoken, " you are going to say that the People have waited long enough, and have a right to be impatient. I know. A right, perhaps, but it's no good to insist on a right that won't work. A woman has a right to marriage, but that doesn't justify her or give her happiness if she makes a bad one. The People may have been duped and disappointed, but the time for impatience and de-structive aggression never comes ; it is of no more value than a burst of temper, it's a waste of time because, in the end, the wisdom of mankind always goes back on it ; the continuity of history is too strong, you can't break it. And that continuity consists in a series of rebirths ; mankind renews itself by the natural process of regeneration from father to son, from father to son. You don't kill the father if you want a son to be born. And, like it or not, the System you hate is the father of any system that can follow it. Why do you speak as if history were a series of disconnected cataclysms ? Do you imagine that the Almighty will serve your turn by creating a fresh Adam and Eve every thirty years ? If you want a new race of men, you have to breed it from the existing stock. There have been revolutions which, though accompanied by violence, have been part of the process of breeding, but the violence has never been the essential and fruitful part of them. Nothing new and enduring comes except out of the old by unbroken inheritance." He turned suddenly to the window and spoke away from his listeners, in a lower and swifter speech, as though what he had to say now were being forced from him by a pressure of personal experience. " And it's true of individuals as it is of communities ; men may be reborn, they may *become* as little children, but not by self-destruction ; ' become ' is the key-word. They may die to their former selves but not until their new self has emerged ;

Paul sprang from a living Saul, not a dead one, and unless I misread the epistles," he added in a voice which suggested that he was smiling, " Paul carried with him always the body of that death."

It was soon after this that Richard became actively observant of an unexplained stress in the life of the Water House. From his first evening, when Rydal had broken in upon his discovery of the portrait, he had been aware that stress existed, but it had seemed well enough explained by a natural sadness in the loss of so young a wife and by Carey's resemblance to her. Now he perceived that Rydal was held in a tension that grief alone did not account for — a tension, moreover, from which his daughter's company was his only release. He exercised great care not to be possessive of her and spoke sometimes with acceptance of the time that must come in which she would marry and leave him, but Richard heard the note of dread within his gallant and accepting tone. Her presence was to him more than a loving companionship — it was his protection against himself, an element in his sanity.

One night, when the two men were sitting beside the fire reading, Rydal looked up and said : " She isn't here, Richard. She's as much absent as if she were dead. But I know she is in that room above, alive, sleeping. I often look in as I go up and watch her breathing." And he added after a pause : " Is it wrong, do you think ? "

" Wrong ? "

" To put all your eggs in one basket ? " He answered his own question. " For the second time in my life . . . What fools the wiseacres are who say one ought to be warned and not repeat one's mistakes ! May be true of the little things that don't matter, but the great mistakes are always repeated — must be — they are part of a man's nature. If it's a question of a few eggs and only a few — those, I dare say, you can dispose of cautiously ; but when it's *all* your eggs — in the end, it's always the same basket."

He was then so near to speaking of his wife that Richard was silent, waiting for him to speak, but he did not, and so it always was, morning or evening, in the house or when they shared a car on the road to Glazeden — always, within the plain happiness of Rydal's actual life, was a tension binding him to the past that denied him the natural relief of speech. Only in Carey's presence was the unacknowledged influence of the portrait lifted from him.

At the back of the house were a vegetable garden and a grassy orchard sloping down to a stream. As spring advanced, Carey would often carry her book or her sewing to a wooden seat cut into a bank near the water. If Richard came home before night, he would glance through the library window to see whether Rydal was still at work and sometimes lean against the sill to talk to him. Often Rydal would treat his coming as a time-signal and stretch himself at his desk, saying he had done enough. Then they would carry a decanter of sherry and four glasses across the orchard. On other occasions, Richard would go on alone and Rydal follow when he had reached a period in his writing or ended the chapter he was reading. The fourth glass was for Mrs. Seaton, a neighbour who, though of Rydal's generation and a lifelong friend of his, was, in her own right, Carey's friend also. Their difference of age, a difference of temperament too, seemed to bind rather than to separate them. Carey being the simpler, Helen Seaton the more ironic, they found much to laugh at in each other and approached by different routes many values and opinions held in common. Mrs. Seaton had become a widow at thirty and had not remarried. It was her frequent habit to come to the Water House near the end of an afternoon and to return across the meadows to her own home before dinner.

Richard began to look forward to finding the girl and the woman together or Carey alone, for thus he saw Carey in two aspects. With Helen Seaton she was gay and quick; alone more serious, with a steadier continuity in discussing a particular subject and a gentle confidence in speaking of herself — of her faiths and hopes, above all of her childhood — which Mrs. Seaton's presence a little restricted.

"You see," Carey explained with a smile, "she has heard all my stories before. She knows almost more about the events of my life than I do myself."

"About the events — but not about you?"

"Oh, I'm not sure," she replied. "I am not particularly hard to know about. Except Father, she probably knows me as well as anyone. But then, you see, she knew Mother — and that, so to speak, gets in the way."

"Because you are so like her?"

"That too, I suppose. But that isn't what I meant."

The May day had cooled suddenly and she drew up over her shoulders the coat she had let fall about her on the wooden seat. She said to Richard: "I don't want to go indoors yet, do you? Will you come for a walk with me? We can leave the sherry here in case Father comes down and pick it up on the way home. . . . Why are you smiling?"

It was a question which, if another had asked it, he might have evaded, but to her he replied: "At the way you said: 'Will you come for a walk?' Like a child asking an older man — a very much older man," he threw in, " whether he will play a game with her. Just a question — not expecting ' yes,' not expecting ' no.' "

" I'm sorry," she said, " if that hurt you," and as they came to the bridge across the small stream she put her arm in his and, without knowing it, emphasized the interval of years between them by saying : " I don't feel at all a child. But there's something," she added, " that I do want to ask you."

" What is it ? "

" Straight out ? "

" Straight out."

" When you came here, were you very unhappy ? . . . No, that's not the real question. I know you were. But you are happier now. Is that true ? "

" Yes, my dear, very true."

She released his arm and walked beside him in silence ; then turned her head and looked at him and turned away. He had seen in her face, not indeed unhappiness nor confusion of mind, but that awareness which he remembered in his own early years — an awareness, now for the first time discovered, of the crowding in upon her of common experience, so that she walked no longer, in the privilege of extreme youth, alone with her private gods.

Not wishing to intrude upon her or say any word

that might embarrass her by its too personal gratitude, he said that the reason for his being happier than he had been was simple enough. His work enthralled him as he had not expected it to do. "I may not be operating, which is work without race or creed or country, and I may, instead, be doing a narrower and certainly a less humane job. But it happens to be one that lets me use the skill of my own hands ; it's not trade, it's not even administration, and that is something for a man trained as a surgeon."

"Yes," she answered, "of course that also is true."

The word "also" and the emphasis upon it were unexpected.

"What else is true, Carey ? "

"Well," she said, "happiness doesn't depend only on what you *do*. I mean : not on actions or happenings, not chiefly on them. People say : ' If only I could get that job ' — or ' if only I could live in the country, not in a town ' — then I should be happy. Or they say that if they had more money or if they had a child, then they would be happy. And now sometimes they believe that, when peace comes again, all the causes of their unhappiness will vanish. I don't believe it's ever true. The thing works the other way round. It's not the outside things that make *you* happy ; it's something inside you that makes *them* seem good or bad. It varies, I mean, even from day

to day. There are days when everything is dull ;
other days when everything glows and shines, special
days — the air smells different, even a horse you meet
in a field looks different and somehow benevolent."
She paused, smiling, at the word, and looked up to see
whether Richard was laughing at her. " And there
are quieter days," she continued, " when the same
kind of thing happens but in a different way. Then
it's not that the smell of the air is sweeter and everything full of gaiety, but that the evil things lose their
power — even the war — and you wake in the
morning and sleep at night knowing——"

He waited, but she did not continue. " Go on,"
he said.

" Knowing," she answered with hesitation, " what
you knew as a child, when you went to bed by day-
light in summer and the room was dark and silent
with big shadows, but you weren't shut in by the
darkness and silence. You were in the garden still
and heard the stream and the movement of birds in
the hedge, and there was no evil."

" You felt that, Carey, and still feel it ? "

" And you ? "

" I remember it," he answered, " when my mother
was alive. It came to me sometimes through her."

" When she died, how old were you ? "

" Twelve."

⟨ 41 ⟩   D

"Twelve," Carey repeated. "Then you knew her. You had her all your childhood."

She asked him to tell her of his mother and allowed him to pass over no detail that his memory would yield. While he spoke, they came near to Mrs. Seaton's house and cut across its fields to strike a road that would bring them home. The sun, reappearing beneath the lower edge of a cloud-bank that had concealed it, flowed across the earth, casting long, tranquil shadows from tree and hedge-row, emphasizing each roughness of the ground, gilding leaf and thorn ; and Richard, while he described his own childhood, imagined hers on such an evening as this when, as she had said, there had been for her " no evil," when she had been pervaded by a knowledge of the essential innocence of created things, a knowledge, communicated to him by his mother for a few years, but since lost. That the girl at his side had acquired this knowledge not from another but of herself, that she retained it scarcely as knowledge at all but as part of her nature was the origin of her power to give rest to her father's perturbed spirit and, now, to his own. But the very young are deeply vulnerable. To allow his love for her, which he now acknowledged within himself, to be spoken, would be to make a claim upon her that their lives could not satisfy ; she would pity, concede, give comfort, for she was fond of him ; she might yield, for she was alone and waking, and he knew his power ; but his was a generation different from hers in more than the years that divided them. This was his second war ; after it, there would be for him no starting again, only a continuance to the end of a life already doubly broken ; but for her it would become an incident of her youth, a point of departure from which her life would stretch ahead, still limitless, still expectant of an ordered fulfilment.

He asked : " Have you ever been to France ? "

" Never."

" Or Italy ? "

" No. Why ? "

" All new," he said. " All to come. Nothing for contrast. Nothing to forget. Everything will be fresh to you — even after this. That is why——"

" But you have had it," she answered. " Nothing can take that from you. And if you are at peace in yourself, will the outside things matter ? Everything will be as fresh to you as to me. Besides," she added, " your life has roots."

" Roots ? "

" Your mother." She drew breath and compelled herself to say : " You see, it's not only that mine died when I was a baby, but that I don't know anything about her. Except the portrait, of course."

" Why that dress, Carey ? "

" The seventeenth-century dress ? Hasn't Father told you ? "

" No. I don't ask him about the portrait."

She nodded in understanding and made no comment. " You see," she said, " Father became a prisoner of war soon after his marriage, and Mother lived here alone. I was born here."

" In which room, Carey ? "

" In which room ? Why ? In the room that looks out over the front lawn. Above the dining-room. Father's room communicates with it. Have you never been into it ? I go sometimes. It is empty except——" A puzzled look appeared in her face but vanished as she continued swiftly : " In the attic, wrapped up, are the pieces of a four-poster that may have belonged there. It must be strange, if you're a man, not to be there — not to be within reach, I mean — when your own child is born. Father didn't see me until I was nearly two. Then, on the first Armistice Day — 1919, I suppose — he and Mother drove over to a ball at Findon and she wore that costume. Afterwards she was painted in it. In the spring they went to France for a holiday. She died there."

" Where ? "

" They were at a little place beyond Hyères. There were pinewoods near the shore. Sometimes they went into Cannes. The place was called Le Lavandou."

" Was your mother buried there ? "

Carey looked at him in surprise. " Why ? Do you think they should have brought her home ? " Then, with flattened tone, as though she were repeating a lesson long, long stale in her mind, she said : " I asked Father that once. I remember I asked what were her favourite flowers. And he said : ' Why ? Do you think I should have brought her home ? ' "

" Does it matter, Carey ? "

" I suppose not. But I should like to know what her flowers were."

" Has your father never told you ? "

" I should like to know that," she repeated, over-riding the question. " And to see her handwriting. Or something she wore when she was alive. Or something she used."

" Mrs. Seaton could tell you about her."

Carey shook her head. " I am too like her, I suppose. I told you — somehow that gets in the way. Helen *does* tell me. I mean, she doesn't refuse, of course. I have asked her sometimes. She told me, for instance, that my mother sang, but when I asked what songs, she couldn't remember."

" Perhaps," Richard said, " that old piano in the sitting-room was hers ? "

"No. I asked. At least, Helen said it wasn't, and why should she tell an untruth about that?"

They had broken away from the road and were in a meadow-track that would bring them to the bridge over the stream. Rydal and Helen Seaton were in the place they had left.

"How did we miss her?" Carey said. "She must have been in the village and come up from there."

Richard made up his mind that, if he could do nothing else for the girl, he could at least find out from Mrs. Seaton, when he was alone with her, what Mrs. Rydal's flowers had been and what songs she had sung.

"I am tired," Carey said.

"Near home," he answered.

She had stopped unaccountably and he had supposed that she was about to sit on the grass. "No," she said, "that's foolish, I suppose, when we are so near. I am not so tired as that," and she compelled herself to go on.

"What is it, Carey?"

She smiled. "Nothing. One of those things. If I'm so like her, when Father and Helen see me in the distance like this— Do you think they speak of her between themselves when they are together? . . . Or not?"

At the bridge she added: "You see, she was

Mother's friend really. I was named after her. She was a Miss Carey."

On the other side of the stream, a turn of the path, which enclosed a little peninsula of birch trees, hid them momentarily from the others. Mrs. Seaton had waved at their approach — a gesture, Richard thought, not of welcome only but of eagerness, almost of excitement, as though she had news to give them. Carey had not seen it and he was glad. The quiet of that instant would abide in his mind; he was reluctant to go forward, and went forward.

The shelter of the birch trees having gone, there was Helen Seaton on her way to them. She had to say, in a brisk, even voice, from which excitement was carefully ironed out, that the Germans had attacked Holland and Belgium.

PART TWO

"I knew Seraphina ; Nature gave her hue,
  Glance, sympathy, note, like one from Eden.
  I saw her smile warp, heard her lyric deaden ;
    She turned to harlotry ; — this I took to be new."

EDMUND BLUNDEN

PART TWO

THE days that followed Germany's opening of the summer campaign of the year Forty gave to all personal experience a cutting edge that it had not had in England since the Armada was sighted. As soon as it became certain that the line was broken, that it could not be reformed, that Weygand could produce no effective counter-attack, that the British and Belgian armies with a part of the French were indeed cut off, there fell upon those summer days that intensity of observation which was given to the Elizabethans by the perilous uncertainty of their lives ; and the more familiar the thing experienced — the steady chime of a clock, the heat of a sunlit wall under the hand, the sound of a distant train — the more highly was it charged by the extremity of danger. Every good thing became more precious ; even things that were, in themselves, neither good nor bad—an account-book lying on the table, a packet of old letters in a drawer—became extraordinary because they were inanimate, because they had existed before the break and lay in their places, still unconscious of it. There was a stab of wonder in every carefree movement of a bird, in the stream's unbroken continuity, in the aloof and unswerving process of Nature.

At Glazeden, Richard and Flower, Chard and Walter Loose, chose, where they could, work that would throw them into company. It was Flower who had the rashness or the courage to say what was in all their minds : that they might be wasting their time. Before their labour came to maturity, the chance to use the instruments they were designing might be gone. No one denied it ; it was evidently true ; but they continued to work ; for the events in Europe, which had given to private feeling a microscopic nearness and enlargement, had, at the same time, lengthened the perspective of impersonal endeavour. Because the security of to-morrow was gone, the long, binding compulsion of past and future took possession of the English mind. Not to yield ceased to be heroic because to yield had become impossible. The armies recovered from Dunkirk had lost their equipment, the Home Guard was an ungrown child, the coasts were unfortified, the Air Force was outnumbered ; only the Navy remained. In country villages, improvised barriers were thrown across the roads ; sign-posts that might direct the enemy were torn down ; and foreign observers smiled with good reason at the lateness and inadequacy of these preparations. The English, too, smiled at them, but never as marks of an end. The threat was recognized, the probability even of great disaster, but never the finality of that disaster if it should come. There arose among the people a stubborn and ancestral madness which, carrying them beyond their urgent fear, enabled them to see these days as already in retrospect. They did not doubt that the time would come in which they or their children would say : " The enemy did not land " or " The enemy landed but in the end we got rid of him." So they built their wooden barriers in West Sarley and Sarley Down, knowing they might fail before Saturday, but knowing also that this would not affect the issue in three or five or twenty or a hundred years. Because to-morrow was breaking like a tidal wave over their heads, they fell back upon their history.

In those weeks of stress, when the enemy was occupying the ports of France and stretching out towards the Seine, Richard had the consolation of working as a member of Research Unit Seven ; Henry Rydal had not, and it was harder then to work alone than in company. Nevertheless, he steadily pursued his task of legal history and shut himself into his library each morning at the same hour. " But sometimes," Carey told Richard, " Father comes out of the library as he never did before, and comes into the sitting-room or the garden — wherever I am — and works on his knee." This was the only outward sign that Rydal was feeling the strain. In the evenings, when the three of them were together and they heard the news bulletins and talked of the day's events, he neither concealed the perilous truth from himself nor was shaken by it.

Then, suddenly, he changed. In the early days of June, when the armies were coming out of Dunkirk, he went to London one morning and came back in the evening a different man.

Richard had chosen this day as his day off and blamed himself for having done so, but by the time he discovered that his host would be absent the arrangement could not be changed. After an early breakfast, he walked to the garage with Rydal, saw him off on his way to the station, and returned to the lawn. There he read peacefully for a great part of the morning until Helen Seaton came in through the gate in the wall. She would have left him undisturbed and gone on into the house to find Carey, but there was in him at that time a desire for companionship ; all the morning Carey had not come out to the lawn as he had hoped, and he gave Mrs. Seaton the chair beside his own. She asked what he was reading. He waved a hand over half a dozen books spread on the grass at his feet.

"Nothing very continuously. Anything to keep my nose out of a newspaper." He handed her an open book, marking a place with his thumb. "Look. Henry dug this out yesterday evening and read it to us — we had been talking about the possible length of the war. It is Drake's prayer on the day he sailed into Cadiz."

Mrs. Seaton could not read without glasses. She returned the book to him and he read :

"' O Lord God, when thou givest to thy servants to endeavour any great matter, grant us also to know that it is not the beginning, but the continuing of the same, until it be thoroughly finished, which yieldeth the true glory ; through him that for the finishing of thy work laid down his life, our Redeemer, Jesus Christ.' "

He was surprised by Mrs. Seaton's comment. "Henry," she said, " has always been an extraordinary creature. He has a great and original candour. He faces facts, understands them, never distorts them or makes them *fit* his ideas. But it remains true that he is much less interested in facts for their own sake than as illustrations of ideas. In that, I have always imagined that Cecil Rhodes was like him — a man of action interested not in action but in the ideas behind action. That is why Henry is so calm in this crisis. No one else could write legal history at such a time." She

spoke as if his calmness irritated her. " It has been like
that all his life."

" Do you mean that he has always been calm ? "

" Good heavens, no. Calm ! I have seen him mad.
But only when an idea has gone bad on him. Dunkirk,
all that is happening, hasn't reversed or contradicted
or perjured — ' perjured ' is his own word — his idea
of the English people. On the contrary. Invasion
wouldn't — even successful invasion. He doesn't
claim that they are invincible." She closed her lips,
smiled and added : " Only that they are immortal.
The Continuing People — not the English only, the
French too, the Americans also, all free peoples ; it is
the absence of the will to liberty that kills — men,
nations, women. So he says."

Richard's mind echoed the words : " men, nations,
women." What was wrong with them ? It took him
a moment to remark their peculiar order. Chance,
presumably. Anyhow, he didn't understand it, and
let it go.

" You knew him," he asked, " in the last war ? "

" A little. Chiefly afterwards."

This was Richard's opportunity. " What was
Mrs. Rydal like ? "

" Extremely beautiful."

" I meant, in character. Her portrait is on the wall,
but I have none in my mind."

"She wasn't easy to define," Mrs. Seaton answered in the easy, conversational tone of one who wished it to be understood that nothing was being concealed. After this non-committal statement, she picked up a book, let its pages turn under her thumb, and was clearly about to comment on it by way of diversion.

"It is an interesting face," Richard intervened.

"Which?"—as if she had forgotten.

"Mrs. Rydal's. . . . Why, I wonder, does Carey know so little about her mother?"

"Naturally. She was a baby at the time."

"Still," Richard persisted, "there's usually a surviving legend."

Mrs. Seaton shrugged her shoulders and twisted the rings on her neat, finely creased hand. "It distresses Henry to be reminded——"

"Of a fact? Her death is a fact. It is unlike him not to face it. After all," Richard added, "death isn't — what was the word? — isn't a 'perjury' of his idea of her; and I should have supposed that, the more because he loved her, he would have told Carey what songs her mother sang."

"But, bless you, Mr. Cannock, why should he remember what her songs were?"

Though warned by a certain asperity in her tone that he was on dangerous ground — perhaps because he had been warned — Richard could not resist saying : " But why should he forget ? "

"In any case," Mrs. Seaton replied with urbane recovery of poise, " it isn't a subject of much importance," leaving Richard to tell himself, without conviction, that perhaps he was, after all, making a mountain out of a molehill. Mrs. Rydal had died nearly twenty years ago. Wasn't it natural that the memory of her should have faded ? The explanation was, in common sense, more reasonable than the questioning in his mind, but the questioning persisted. He could not escape from two facts : that Mrs. Seaton did avoid, with evident embarrassment, the subject of Mrs. Rydal, and that Carey had seen nothing her mother had worn, no ring, no brooch, no piece of lace, nothing that had belonged to her, no word in her handwriting. This might have been unimportant if Carey herself had not been troubled by it, but he could not forget her hungry listening to his account of his own mother or her expression of puzzled loss when she had said that she was without roots.

That afternoon, he had an inclination to report to her his failure with Mrs. Seaton. He might say : "Well, it's true, Carey ; she seems to have forgotten your mother's songs," but, when these words had already taken shape in his mind, he looked at Carey and decided not to speak them. Why ? Because they would disturb her ? Not for that reason only. He had to recognize that he avoided the subject for his own sake ; in touching it, he did not know what it was he touched.

He and Carey dined alone. There was no word from her father. This was unusual. The routine of his visits to London was established, for he went to consult books, and libraries closed early ; he ordinarily returned by a train that enabled him to reach the house soon after seven. At half-past, Carey telephoned to the station. The train had not been late ; it had come and gone ; Mr. Rydal had not been on it. Carey rang for Mrs. Durrant and said that she and Mr. Cannock would not wait. Mr. Rydal could now come only by the slow train ; he would not reach the house until after ten.

The garden was warm after dinner and so still that the flame under their coffee burned straight. Carey lay back in her chair, her face turned a little away so that less than her full profile was visible, and asked, as she had not before, what progress Richard was making at Glazeden. The nature, even the purpose, of his experiments was unknown to her, and for an instant he supposed with astonishment that she was about to put to him questions that he must not answer ; but it was not so ; she was genuinely incurious of secrets ; the word " Glazeden " had fallen by chance ; and it appeared to his surprise that all she wanted was that he should somehow talk of himself — past, present, future, it made no matter, so long as it was of himself that he talked. While he obeyed, she watched him, smiles coming and going on her face, extremely various smiles, now of amusement, now of a compassionate tenderness that puzzled him, now — under eyes momentarily closed — of simple happiness ; and, when he was silent, there was between them an acceptance of the long interval so perfectly at ease, so intimate, that Richard, seeing under her fallen lashes the gleam of a tear, had no need to acknowledge it except by a touch of his hand on hers. Her eyes opened ; her smile instantly returned.

" But it is, in a way, frightening," she said, " on this particular day of all days, to be happier than you have ever been."

He was always to recall, in the light of what followed, that these words, as though he had been a partaker of the thought from which they sprang, were at once fully comprehensible to him ; he also had known that " this particular day " now over and this crystal evening were a point of departure to be, in the future, accurately remembered. He began deliberately to engrave upon his mind certain present details — the luminous plane of whiteness that a trick of the dusk had laid upon the side of Carey's throat, the smell of mown grass from the barrow the gardener had left, the sharp, metallic gleam and shadow of the creeper that stood up about the dining-room window. He had risen as he touched her hand and now stood in front of her chair, facing the house.

She asked : " What time is it ? "

He answered : " Eight minutes to ten."

From his wrist-watch, his eyes moved on to the house again, first on to the dining-room window, then to the window above it. All others in the house had been blacked out, but this had not, for the room was unoccupied ; and the panes, curtainless, gave back to the rooky dusk a polished interior darkness. Within their frame appeared at that instant a human movement which his reason accounted for with the name of Mrs. Durrant, who, no doubt, had entered Mrs. Rydal's room to look for something there. But for what ? Since Carey had spoken of it, he had visited the room ; except that a round gilt mirror was still hanging above the mantelpiece, it was empty to the boards ; and, even if Mrs. Durrant had business in it, why at this hour and by what light ? Nevertheless he did not doubt his eyes ; someone had moved and gone ; and he supported the comfortably rational explanation of " Mrs. Durrant " by saying to himself : she will have forgotten that the windows are uncurtained; the silly woman will strike a light. But she did not; in his heart he had known that she would not; he stood at gaze, believing and not believing that she was there; and when again and yet again the interior darkness was crossed by a paler movement, now unquestionably not of Mrs. Durrant's heavy form, the rational explanation slid from him — that is to say, was not wrenched from him by any tremor of fear — and finding himself, on the third occasion, looking up into a girl's face, he recognized her without shock and without remembrance of her having been dead twenty years.

Her left hand travelled across her breast; it was laid on the opposite shoulder at the naked curve of the throat springing, and moved and moved there, the fingers gripping and releasing, as though, hesitant and lost and seeking, she found reassurance in this touch upon herself. The hand fell away; first head then body was turned away; she moved, was gone — gone, for the word " vanished " did not in his mind apply to her; he had as yet no sense of her being spectral, only of having seen what was naturally there if you had eyes to see it; and her disappearance from his sight gave him nothing at first but the plainly consequent thought that, since she had turned to her right, she was moving from window to door. A little twist of passage from the door of that room would bring her to the stair-head. It was the imagining of her on the stairs that pierced him at last.

He saw her as wandering there, her hand flat, feeling the dark wall, and what possessed him was neither dread of her approach — even though she should emerge into the garden — nor any chill of visitation from the grave, for death had no part in his thought of her, but compassion for her evident and extreme loneliness, for an anguish of the soul in her that he felt but could not define — for her lostness, he might have said; and this compassion, which had the character of love itself and burned him and drew the night air in sudden gust to the back of his throat, he felt not for the sake of her likeness to Carey, nor for her own personal sake, but — and here he was caught in the icy wonder of being invaded and possessed by a spirit external to his critical self — for the sake of her assured redemption. Whatever sin she had committed or was about to commit was already pardoned, though she did not know it; whatever she had done or might do was not to be condemned; what she had lost was found. But she was wandering on the stair: he could not tell her this, and suddenly he lost his own sense of it, he began to disbelieve what he had seen and known, his heart was emptied out as though he had been walking on the water and were now sinking.

Carey had remarked nothing in his stillness and silence. She rose and said that if they walked a little way down the lane they would meet her father's car returning, and lifted her hand towards his arm, assuming that he would come with her across the lawn; but he could not; he put his arms about her and held her as though she had been dead and were alive again; then stood away and led her towards the house. "Let us go in and wait for your father there." She followed him through the door by which he had first entered the house and into the little hall at the foot of the stairs where, on that winter's night, Rydal had called out: "Carey, we have a guest"; and now Richard opened its door that Carey might go in ahead of him. When he followed, none but she was there. She seated herself on the piano-stool and looked up at him, her breath calm, her eyes steady.

"Richard, what are you looking for?"

He answered a different question: "This quiet room!"

"Quiet," she repeated, and, turning to the piano, struck a chord on it and listened, and struck another and listened; then began to sing. Suddenly, through the open window on her left hand, from behind the heavy curtains that masked it, Henry Rydal's voice interrupted them, crying:

"Who is that singing? Answer. Who is it?"

The latch of the outer door was violently lifted ; he came, with a stooping plunge, from the hall into the room and there straightened himself to the rigidity of a man about to fall in some dreadful seizure ; his heels were raised from the ground, his neck was stretched from his collar, his fingers dragged at the loosened ends of his tie.

" It is you, Carey ! "

" Yes, Father, who else should it be ? "

He took her hands and held them against his face. Having gazed at her long and searchingly, he said : " I am sorry, my darling. I heard the music as I crossed the lawn. I didn't know— It didn't enter my mind— I have been——" At this he broke off, stared at Richard, then turned to Carey again. " I have been occupied——" But he had forgotten what he was about to say and ended with a gesture of help-lessness.

He was persuaded to sit down. Richard went into the dining-room and returned with brandy. Henry Rydal took it and drank.

" Well, what news from Glazeden ? "

" I haven't been there. You remember, it was my day off."

Rydal shook his head. " I am tired, that's all. Sit here, Carey. . . . No, here, close to me. . . . I shall be all right in a minute. What was that song ? "

She told him. He nodded his head and made no answer. " Of course you are right," he said at last. " Of course it was you singing."

From that day onward, Rydal's visits to London became more frequent. He would go twice or three times in a week, but never on two days consecutively, nor was he absent at night. He was in a condition of profound disquiet. For a great part of the time his intellect was as clear and his talk as energetic as in the past, but his mind would swerve from his subject, he would lose his thread without seeming even to be aware that he had lost it, and lapse abruptly into silence. He was as much dependent on Carey as he had been, hungry for her companionship and appeased by it ; but sometimes, in the midst of conversation with her, his expression changed in response to an obscure shifting of the plane of his thought, and he became curious of her face and stared into it as though he were unsure of her identity. Then, like one who is awakened violently from a dream, he would say : " Carey ? " with an interrogative note, and she would answer : " Yes, Father — Carey " and take his hand to reassure him.

At first she made light of the change and would say only that her father was over-tired. When Richard asked : " What is happening in London ? What is troubling him there?" she said: "Why? His going to London has nothing to do with it!" and he knew that she believed this to be true. Nevertheless, three evenings later, she did say to her father:

"Don't go to London to-morrow."

"Why not?"

"Because you are tired. You will make yourself ill. Stay here and be peaceful."

Unexpectedly he consented, but next morning had forgotten his consent; he came to breakfast in clothes he would not wear unless he were going to London; and Carey's protest was thrust aside.

"How can I get on with my work, child, if I haven't the books?" and he began to explain, with the elaborate plausibility of a lie, that he had reached a stage of his work at which references not available at home were continually needed. Carey knew that he was lying but would not admit it, and there stood between her and Richard a subject on which neither could speak openly to the other.

It was Mrs. Seaton who unexpectedly invited Richard's judgment. On two evenings she had been in the house by chance when Rydal returned from London, and without comment had observed the change in him; on a third she came deliberately and, when night was falling, asked Richard to walk across the fields with her. She had the abrupt way of Englishwomen made confident by their breeding, and the knowledge that to plunge for the truth is often the surest way of surprising it.

" Well," she said, " what do you make of it ? "

" Of Henry ? "

" But, of course."

" I had hoped you would instruct me."

" And why ? I don't live in the house. You do."

" Mrs. Seaton," Richard answered, " why should we fence with each other ? You remember that morning on which I asked you what songs Mrs. Rydal sang and you wouldn't tell me ? "

" Couldn't," she said, " not wouldn't. Why should you think otherwise ? "

" As you please. Then we can't help each other."

His firmness shook her. " Genuinely and truly," she said, " I don't understand. What has this — what has Henry's present behaviour — to do with the songs his wife sang or didn't sing ? "

Richard told her of the occasion on which Carey had been at the piano singing, and her father had thrust his head in at the window, then burst into the room, and had — he paused for the phrase that should communicate to Mrs. Seaton what he himself had felt.

" What ? " she asked.

" He didn't recognize her."

" Didn't recognize Carey ? "

" It wasn't," Richard said, " that he didn't recognize her features, of course. It was the oddest thing to stand there and watch them as I did — to feel his mind working. He knew her — and didn't know her." The effort needed to make himself say more was so great that Richard fell back upon a smooth formality of words, an easy flatness. " I received the impression," he said, " that Henry expected to find someone else, and the shock of finding — well," he added with a grin of relief, " sherry and vermouth ! They look alike but their tastes are different. You pour out what you suppose to be a glass of sherry. You put it to your lips with the expectation of sherry in your mind. And it isn't. And the other taste——"

Mrs. Seaton let his words fall into silence. They had passed through the open meadows into the wood that was an approach to her garden. Beyond the trees' darkness Richard would have turned back, but she invited him into her house and lighted an oil-lamp in her drawing-room.

" Mr. Cannock," she began, " there is a reason that we should be frank with each other. Until lately that house was one of the happiest — no, perhaps not *happiest* ; Henry has never been happy since he lost Venetia — but certainly one of the most peaceful I have ever known. Now that is changed. It affects me because I love the girl. Do you resent my saying that I believe it affects you for the same reason ? In any case," she pursued steadily before he had time to answer, "it affects you because the girl loves you. You know that ? Or are you blind to it ? "

" What she feels for me," Richard answered, " is, quite rightly, the affection of——"

" No," Mrs. Seaton interrupted, " not ' of a child,' if that is what you were going to say."

" Very well," he answered with a smile, " what I was going to say was, perhaps, foolish. The truth is harder. Carey is a woman — grant that — and I won't make a parade of saying that a man is necessarily ruled out because he happens to be more than twenty years older than she is. But I am ruled out nevertheless."

" By what ? "

" Quite simply, Mrs. Seaton, by her goodness."

" ' Goodness ' ? That's a plain word not often used plainly. Are you so evil, then ? "

" No, but I am sceptical. I am set. She has a special innocence. I don't know how to put it except by saying that she has a quiet mind, an inward peace that continually renews her. I have not. I should have to be reborn, and I have become incapable of it. As for my loving her or her loving me, the word has so many meanings that it's best in our case not to speak it ; it would have different meanings for her and for me. No," he repeated, "the thing is impossible. Not for the obvious conventional reasons. Not because I am 'too old for her.' Not because she is 'too good for me.' I haven't that kind of modesty. But I have become incapable of miracles and hers are ahead of her."

Mrs. Seaton raised her head to continue the argument, then forbore. The mind, she knew, is often bound by what the lips speak; she did not wish this man, whom she liked and who so evidently lacked the self-confidence that makes easy the offering and the acceptance of love, to make his own way more difficult. Her feeling was that Carey, though certainly she had more than affection for him, might prove, in the end, not 'to love him enough' — by which she meant not enough to enable him to yield himself to love. He is the type, she thought, that needs to be thawed out; for, in spite of her intelligence, she had a habit of thinking in types, of putting mankind into neat categories, and she had failed to discern that what held Richard back was by no means a need to be thawed but a genuinely intuitive fear that the resulting avalanche might sweep Carey out of herself, out of her quietness of mind, into — what? He didn't know. In this, as nowadays in so much else, he didn't see the end of the tunnel.

" The odd thing is," he said, " that I can't for the

life of me remember how we came to be talking of that rather unprofitable subject."

"The point is this," Mrs. Seaton answered. "Whatever it is that is happening to Henry is affecting Carey. And Carey, as you yourself said just now, has — you called it 'an inward peace,' I think. Am I right?"

Richard answered, "Yes," smiling at her tone's brisk repudiation of personal responsibility for the phrase.

"Very well. Now, it needs a great deal to disturb that 'inward peace.' She's extraordinary in that way. Happenings that would throw other people out of their stride don't affect her——"

"Unless," Richard interrupted, "they are concerned with her mother."

"Really, Mr. Cannock, you have an obsession about her mother. Something in London is upsetting Henry; something, as far as one can judge, that happens each time he goes there. How can it conceivably have anything to do with Venetia?"

"And yet," Richard answered, "it has, you know."

"What grounds have you for that?"

He was determined now and pursued her steadily. "First, the effect on Carey. Then the pretty obvious one that, when Henry's at his worst — for example, when he came in that evening of which I told you

and found that it was Carey who had been singing —
there is always a confusion of the same kind — a half-
and-half confusion of identity. Isn't it clear that Mrs.
Rydal is pressing on his mind?" He looked Mrs.
Seaton full in the face and came out with : "Whatever
happens in London reminds him of her."

Mrs. Seaton, who did not easily flinch, turned clean
away. With her back to him she said : "That is
impossible." Then, facing him again, she added :
"You must put that from your mind. You must put
it altogether from your mind."

"And the alternative ?"

"To be frank — some woman ?"

Richard answered : "You don't believe that."

"No," she admitted. "You are right. I don't."

It is always hard to know when and under what
impulse a suspicion first presented itself. Certainly it
was not until now that Richard, in his mind, gave
words and recognition to the idea, of which he was
never afterwards able to mark down the precise origin,
that Henry Rydal had killed his wife. That once
accepted, everything suddenly fell into place, everything plausibly explained itself : his avoidance of
the subject, the fascination the portrait had for him, his
compensating love of Carey, his delight and agony in
her resemblance to the woman who was dead. It was
natural that he should wish to put away every re-

membrance of her — her handwriting, her jewels, her lace, all that had been hers except the portrait — the single, self-tormenting, inescapable exception. Mrs. Seaton's reticence, if she was shielding him for his sake or her own or Carey's, was natural too. And now, in London, the truth was threatening him. Begging, bribing, concealing, he was at the mercy of one or more than one who knew and could prove it. Everything fitted except one thing — Henry Rydal's own nature, the extraordinary gentleness and refinement of it. Thinking of his friend, Richard would have liked to believe him incapable of murder ; yet now, in bitter reason, he accepted the possibility. The look of fear in Mrs. Seaton's face endorsed it.

While Richard was working in the laboratory next day, Flower was suddenly moved to throw in scornful comment on the surrender of France, for Flower had a dislike of the French and their refusal of the Prime Minister's offer of union with England had been a relief to him.

" Lord," he said, " if they'd accepted we should have been in a pretty mess ! It's like a man who offers marriage to try to keep his girl when she is ratting. When she *has* ratted, he offers up little prayers of thanksgiving at breakfast each morning. I knew a man once who——"

But that story, like Mamillius's, was never told. Flower chattered in an undertone when work was going smoothly ; encountering a difficulty, he sucked in his underlip, gripped it with his teeth, and attacked his problem in stubborn silence. Long afterwards he came up to breathe and gasped out :

"Anyhow, there's one thing about it : no one can say this time that we fought to the last Frenchman."

"No," said Richard, "that at least is true."

"And what isn't, Mr. Cannock ?"

"What you implied — that we are well rid of France. We may win the war without her, which will be good for our pride ; but if we try to make a peace without her, Europe will be like a University that has turned itself into a technical training college."

When work was over, Richard found Henry Rydal in the ante-room, and on their way home together spoke to him of France and of Flower's attitude of mind.

"I know, I know," Rydal said. "But the real question, in the end, isn't one of political advantage or national pride. The root question isn't whether France is whipped but whether, in the end, she learns to kiss the rod and begins to whine and to sentimentalize her surrender — not whether she loses her liberty for the time being but whether she tries to justify herself by repudiating it. Comfort, order, babies, nests — all the German sentimentalities of cannon fodder or, if you like, every woman's excuse for selling herself — when Vichy begins to yap about those things and about the generosity of her captor, then even France will begin to stink in the grave ! "

What Rydal said was not inconsistent with his former way of thought ; he had always believed passionately in the independence of the French genius and spoken of France as if she were a woman of high mettle ultimately incapable of betraying the principle of her own freedom ; but now his manner of speech, even on this subject, had in it a new wildness, a note of bitterness foreign to him, and Richard was glad, when they reached the Water House, to find Carey awaiting them. But she herself had less influence on her father than in the past. At dinner, he asked suddenly what day it was — Tuesday ?

" Tuesday," she said.

" Then I must go to London to-morrow."

He said it with a little sigh of extreme weariness ; then, the decision made, visibly commanded himself for his daughter's sake to escape from his obsession and plunged into a discussion of the book he had seen open beside her chair in the sitting-room — Shorthouse's *John Inglesant*. Why had she chosen that ?

" Do you remember," she said, " you read it aloud to me — it must have been two years ago ? Why do you never read aloud any more ? "

" I will, my dear, if it would please you."

" But you must enjoy it too ! "

He replied, as though he were speaking of something lost beyond hope of recovery : " I think I should. It's a peaceful thing to do. The trouble is : one can't have long gaps ; reading aloud ought to be pretty regular."

" Why should it not be ? " she answered. " Begin to-night."

Richard had seldom felt so affectionate an admiration for his friend as he did that evening while they sat first in the garden, later in the lamplit room, and that quiet, lively voice read the opening of *Inglesant*. Once, Rydal turned two pages together and overran the break in sense without being aware of it until half a dozen lines had been read ; then, making neither comment nor apology, turned back patiently and continued. Once, near the end of the evening, he let his eyes come up and said :

" I have not told you, Carey. We took this book to France with us, your mother and I, the last time we were together."

Richard had never before heard him speak in this way ; it might be the beginning of relief if he could talk of Mrs. Rydal to Carey ; but he said no more ; he picked up the volume again and pursued his reading.

Richard had ceased to listen. He was watching Carey's face. She was lying on the floor, a cushion under her elbows, her head supported by her hands, staring at the empty hearth. A minute, perhaps more than a minute, had passed before she interrupted :

" Then this is the third time you have read *Inglesant* aloud — if you read it aloud to her."

" We didn't finish," Rydal answered. His eyes returned to the book, but he did not read for a little while. Then suddenly he went on :

" ' And sitting down, he drew Johnny on his knee, and taking from his pocket a small book, he said : " Here, my friend, let us see how you can read this." It was the *Phaedo* of Plato, which Johnny knew nearly by heart, and he immediately began, with almost breathless rapidity to construe with, here and there, considerable freedom, till the gentleman stopped him with a laugh. " Gently, gently, my friend. I saw you were a scholar but not that you were a complete Platonist ! I fear your master is one who looks more to the Divine sense than to the grammar ! But never mind, you and I shall be much together, and——" ' "

Richard was listening now and, as he listened, he became aware that the chair opposite Henry Rydal's, which, while he was intent upon Carey's face, had lain a little beyond the angle of his vision, was occupied. He turned his head and saw there the girl who had looked down upon him from the window, seated with her hands folded in her lap and her head bent forward as though she had long been listening. The effect upon him was not of shock but of a natural continuity and repose. Carey at this moment turned in the direction of the chair but there was no change in her expression, she saw nothing. The reading continued up to the end of the second chapter where the boy, standing at the gateway of the Priory, looked after his father and Eustace as they rode up the hill. At this Henry Rydal closed the book, and Richard, his eyes returning to the opposite chair, found it empty, as it had certainly been when they came in from the garden.

Next evening, the reading pitiably broke down. After his return from London and before dinner, Rydal had taken Carey by the arm and paced up and down the lawn with her, holding her upper arm by reason of his great height, holding and pressing it as though he were striving to communicate to her some desperate appeal. But his head was turned away, he said nothing, and when she spoke gave replies that linked verbally with her questions but did not answer them. At dinner, the subject of France having arisen, he had exclaimed with a ferocity evidently personal : " People can't be saved who won't save themselves ! " and when Carey asked, would he be at home to-morrow, he had answered : " Yes, yes, I shall be at home," and had looked round the room as though it were a prison.

That he was now faced by some final decision Richard could not doubt. To-morrow or the next day, he said to himself, the issue will be forced, and he determined to make — at whatever risk of interference — an attempt to help. To-morrow morning, he would go to Glazeden an hour later than usual ; he would choose the time when Henry ordinarily walked in the garden before settling down in his library, and would say in effect : Tell me. Even if I can do no good, it will make it easier to tell some human being. Perhaps the opportunity to say this might come before the morning if Henry loitered after Carey had gone to bed, and Richard began to turn over in his mind what advice he could give, what advice it was possible to give, to a man who was persuaded to confess himself a murderer. How strange, how impossible it was, that such a confession should be made in this house which had once seemed to him the most peaceful in the world !

After dinner, Carey, with steady determination, took *Inglesant* from its shelf and laid it on her father's knee. Obediently he began to read the third chapter, telling how the Father Sancta Clara, by his teaching, gained in influence over the boy.

" ' He read the classics, making them not dead school books, but the most human utterances that living men ever spoke ; and while from these he drew illustrations of human life when reading Plato — which he did every day — he led his pupil to perceive, as he did more fully when he grew older, that wonderful insight into the spiritual life and spiritual distinctions which even Christianity has failed to surpass. He led him, step by step, through that noble resolve by which Socrates — at frightful odds and with all ordinary experience against him — maintains the advantage to be derived from truth ; he pointed out——' "

The book was lowered. Rydal's hands were spread out over the open pages and he gazed at the chair opposite him.

" Not to-night, Carey," he said, " nothing comes to-night."

He rose, kissed her, touched Richard on the shoulder and said good-night. Carey put her arm in his and went to the door with him.

" Will you turn out the lamps when you come ? " she said to Richard. " I shall not come down again," but after an interval of nearly half an hour she reappeared and stood by the fireplace.

" He will say nothing."

" Have you been with him all this time ? "

She shook her head. " Not at first. I went to my

own room. Then to him. As I expected, he was awake, still dressed, sitting at his small writing-table bolt-upright, his hands on it, like a blind man reading Braille. He said : ' What is it, Carey ? ' I said — I'm not sure of the words — I said wasn't I of any use to him ? Couldn't I be ? He took my hand and held it, but without looking at me. At last he said : ' Not in this. Not yet. Go to bed, my dear. There's nothing I can tell you yet because I myself don't know.' I said : ' Then, Father, it is true — something dreadful is happening ? ' Then he did look at me and answered : ' Nothing may happen. I am afraid nothing will.' "

" ' I am *afraid* nothing will ' ? " Richard echoed. " Were those his words ? "

" Yes."

" And then ? "

" I just went away," Carey answered. " I came down here. I'm frightened, Richard. What shall I do ? . . . Oh, there was one other thing he said. As I was going out of the door, he said : ' I shall go to London again to-morrow.' I think he had that moment made up his mind. Then — I suppose my face must have troubled him — he made a little forward movement ; I thought he was coming across the room to me ; but he didn't. ' I'm sorry, Carey,' he said. ' But perhaps this is the end. After this, one way or the other, probably I shan't go to London again.' "

When she had told this, Carey knelt on the floor beside Richard's chair and took his hand between hers.

" Carey," he said, " what is it you are frightened of — what precisely, I mean ? "

" For him. I feel — when he goes to London — I feel he is terribly alone and——"

" Nothing more definite ? "

She was silent. Because he believed that her suspicion was the same as his, because neither could communicate it to the other, he felt divided from her as if by a wall of glass. Wishing to comfort her, he could find no words of reassurance ; the intimacy that had existed between them was frozen ; and when she rose to her feet, said good-night and went from the room, he let her go. For a long time he did not move. At last he decided to go to bed and extinguished the lamps, first in the sitting-room, then in the hall. He was now in darkness and put his hand in his pocket for a torch. There was none there. Remembering that he had left his torch in the pocket of a light overcoat that he had brought home that day from Glazeden, he went into the closet under the reverse of the stairs in which the coat was hanging. While he was fumbling in the darkness, there was a footstep on the stairs immediately above his head and an intuition stilled him.

The footsteps, which he knew to be Henry Rydal's, were slow and cautious. As they advanced beyond the turn of the stairs, a hand brushed along the wall that was common to staircase and closet. Richard imagined Henry as feeling his way in the dark, and did not stir. The door to the sitting-room was opened ; there was no sound of its being closed again ; and Richard knew certainly that, if ever he would have been right to disclose his presence, the moment of possible disclosure was past. He could not follow Henry into the darkness of the sitting-room nor could he leave the closet and go upstairs without risk of intolerable encounter.

From the sitting-room there came now and then a sound which seemed to be that of furniture being moved ; then, after a period of blankness, a returning footfall. It was slower and heavier than formerly ; it laboured on the stairs, as though each step were being deliberately planted ; it halted — there was an interval of silence — then continued with the same laborious deliberation. It was not until after this that Richard's mind was icily flooded with the knowledge that Henry Rydal had in his arms some heavy burden which could not easily be carried through the narrow passage of the stairs. To know this and yet to have no assurance of what was being carried, to see — as if there were no dividing wall — Rydal's great height stooped forward, his eyes shut against the dark, his lips opened for breath as he strained to his task, and yet to be able to imagine, as enclosed and supported by his arms, no specified thing, cast upon Richard, in the clearness of apprehension which this experience had given him, the contrary stress and entanglement of a dream. When at last the staircase was ascended, he listened in expectation of the footsteps' continuing in the first-floor passage which led to Rydal's own room, but they ceased ; Rydal was waiting and resting ; but the time of waiting contradicted this belief, no man could stand so long with a heavy burden laid across his arms, and suddenly it was borne in upon Richard that the ascent had been continued ; Rydal had proceeded up another flight that led to the attics only. Presently his lightened footstep was again to be heard as he went to his bedroom. His task had been accomplished, his burden set down.

Richard went at once into the sitting-room and examined it under the beam of his torch. It was almost a shock to find nothing visibly disturbed ; if furniture had indeed been moved, it had been replaced. *John Inglesant* lay open at the abandoned page. Richard picked it up, laid in a wooden spill to mark the place, closed it, and, as he laid it down again, observed, in the torch's accidental sweep, that the music-stool was gone. For a moment he was helplessly at a loss ; there was no reason, only something remotely farcical and inexplicable, in this trivial disappearance ; but his curiosity leapt again when he saw what the piano had almost concealed — that the stool, which was very low and stood on gilt legs of wood deeply carved, had been slid under the piano and beyond it and now stood against the wall. His gaze and the torch-beam, travelling up together, came upon a rectangle of unfaded wallpaper from which Mrs. Rydal's portrait had been taken away.

In the morning, when Carey and Richard came to breakfast, Henry Rydal was not in the dining-room.

"If he has overslept," Carey said, "and if he is going to London, I ought to wake him."

She was about to go to her father's room when Richard stopped her.

"I will go."

"Why ?"

"I will go," he repeated.

No one was in Rydal's room. Before returning to Carey, Richard walked out to the garage. She saw him pass the open window of the dining-room but asked no question. Only Richard's car was in the garage. He returned to the house. The telephone was in the dining-room and he must use it in Carey's presence. He telephoned to the station-master. Mr. Rydal had gone up by the early train. His car was in the station yard.

"Carey," Richard said, "have you been into the sitting-room this morning?"

She looked at him, bewildered. "No. Not yet. Why?"

"Your mother's portrait has gone. Your father came down last night and took it away."

Carey shook her head slowly, her lips trembled. Struggling for control, she lost it, tears rolled down her cheeks and she flung up her arm to cover them.

"Carey!" he said; but, before he could come to her, she was gone from the room, and he found her standing before the place where the portrait had been. There, her arm, when he touched it, was rigid; her whole body was taut; until, suddenly, with a little panting cry, she relaxed and turned to him and leaned against him and shook and shook as though in the agony of a fever.

He held her fast, saying nothing. When she was again mistress of herself, she said: "Must you go to work to-day?"

"I must, Carey."

She nodded. "Of course you must."

"If I can, I'll come back early."

At that she smiled and said : " It will be a long time."

He left Glazeden twenty minutes before six o'clock, not for the sake of his promise to Carey but because his work released him. A stubborn difficulty that had long stood in the way of the development of his fighter gunsight, the Paramount, had been overcome. The overcoming of it had been by a method of new principle, not of device, and the principle, when his mind grasped at it, appeared suddenly to be applicable not to his Paramount alone but to the instruments for submarine detection then in use. He had sent at once for Chard and told him what he had hit upon. Chard listened to his outline, fired by the idea implied in it, and squared himself at Richard's table to examine his drawings and calculations ; the thing was promising enough to keep them all night at the exploration of it. But Chard wrenched himself from the drawing under his hand and pushed back his chair.

" Leave it for to-night. Let's sleep on it. Better come to it fresh in the morning."

Richard had nodded. " Good," he said. " So be it. But it's something to sleep on, Chard, I do believe."

Chard grinned. " Probably. One never knows. May be a snag somewhere. Usually is when one gets one's tail up about an idea."

This was at half-past five. Ten minutes later, Richard climbed into his car, the glow of attainment upon him, wrapped in the haze that excludes everything but the new idea at its centre, altogether in the happy mood, familiar since he was a boy, of wishing to be home to brood upon a secret triumph. Then he remembered suddenly to what he might be returning at the Water House. The recollection touched him with the gnawing distress there is sometimes in waking from the reality of a happy and lucid dream to the unreality of life's confused anxieties. At his table with Chard, working upon a problem of science, which had not been made by its naval purpose any less a problem of science, he had forgotten the insane, persistent ruin of civilization. Now a sense of barrenness and dust, of a spreading evil at once stupid and malicious, returned to him with the impact of spiritual despair, to which in a long war men become vulnerable. For this, he knew, there was no remedy in optimism or avoidances ; there was a palliative in courage, but no more ; there was no remedy but in quietness of spirit, for to the spirit that is quiet a natural refreshment comes as to a body that sleeps, but not otherwise. Despair is a disease, an insomnia of the soul that forbids its own healing ; but the quiet of others may give to one in the grip of it an opportunity to be healed. This quiet Richard had found at the Water House when he had first gone there ; it had comforted and enthralled him ; he had loved Carey because of it ; now, in her, it was threatened at its source. In that dark moment, driving through the sunlight of the July evening, thinking of Henry Rydal and the misery that overhung him and must soon declare its nature, Richard was visited by that most bitter of all terrors — the terror not of a single thing that may be defined and encountered, but of the dis-integration of life's good, of a perceived mockery in its smiling appearances. So great was the desolate chill of this contradiction that he stopped his car and watched the good things of the earth — the sun, the lengthening shadows, the cheerful hopping of birds in the hedgerow, the curving of grasses in the little breeze — with a sense of their not belonging to him. Even the recollection of his day's work and his con-versation with Chard, which now slid back into his mind, was barren of comfort. He put away the thought of his emptied triumph as he might have put away a consolatory hand ; then observed, as a spectator, that his car was standing at the roadside, and slid in his clutch and drove on.

At least there was left to him a power of control in the presence of others, and he believed, when he found Carey in the garden, that he communicated to her none of his mood ; instead, he told her that he had

had a good day at Glazeden, that he had seen his way through a difficulty that had long stood in the way of progress ; and she said : " Oh, Richard, I am glad. You have always your work to hold on to. When other things go wrong, that stands."

" Yes," he answered ; but he was repeating a formula from the past ; it had been true of him once and had survived so much that he had believed it would always be true.

" You say it doubtfully," she said. " Isn't it still true ? "

They went together to the familiar place by the stream, carrying with them the decanter of sherry for the reassurance there was in preserving the old routine, and it was not until they had for some time been seated there that Carey broke through the surface of conversation and said :

" In places where one has been happy, it's harder than anything on earth to endure being unhappy as we are now ! . . . I know you are unhappy, Richard. I'm not sure that I know why. You are his friend, but you can't love him as I do. He has been my life. Any good there is in me is — is called out by the good in him. Without him — I mean if he is broken, if——"

" I too feel that, in my own way, Carey. Through you, perhaps. This place has been a heaven to me.

It was sanity, goodness, peace — everything I seemed
to have lost."

" And now have lost again ? " she answered. Then
her voice hardened and quickened. " It's odd. We
sit here. We pretend to each other that Father may
come by the earlier train. He may be here in ten
minutes ! But we know he won't be. Then Mrs.
Durrant will ring the bell. We shall go into dinner.
And we shall pretend that he will come by the later
train. But we know he won't. He will never come.
The thing has happened. I know. He has been
taken away. Father has been taken away ! Why ?
Whatever he did in the past, to punish him now is
only revenge. It does no good. It's meaningless as
a deterrent. Oh, poor Father," she cried, " whatever
it was he did, he had outgrown it ! We had made
a new life together. He was a new man. He *had*
been born again — sanity, goodness, peace : like you,
everything he seemed to have lost. And now she
drags him back into her grave."

The last sentence was spoken with a bitterness that
contradicted all his previous knowledge of Carey, and
she followed it, before he could answer, with a fierce,
passionate question. " Why don't you speak the
truth ? You believe it too. You believe he killed
my mother." Then she covered her face and said
in her own voice, quietly : " That is why I am mad !

That is why I burn inside and can do no good! I hate *her* for it. Do you understand? She has taken him away to the hell where she is. I know that is mad and wicked. I hear my own voice say it, and I know. But all his life, all the years I remember, he has been learning to be at peace *from her*, and now it is all ruined. As if she were alive, she has him again. . . . Well, let us go in. Why should we sit here?"

"Perhaps we are both wrong," Richard said. "Perhaps he will come back."

"Do you believe it?" she asked. "No. . . . Oh, Richard, I'm sorry. Hatred is vile and barren and useless. Anyhow, she is dead."

Mrs. Durrant, uncertain of Rydal's coming, had kept back dinner; it was not ready yet. Richard and Carey went into the sitting-room to wait. Carey knelt on the window-seat, looking out on to the lawn, and Richard stood behind her. On their left, Mrs. Durrant was to be seen now and then moving in and out of the dining-room; on their right, the old red brick of the garden wall, where the shadow of the house did not reach it, glowed in the late sun. The church clock struck half-past seven. Richard had turned back into the room when he heard the creak of the gate, and swung round to the window again.

"Is that your father?"

"Yes," she answered. Then, in a shuddering undertone : " Oh my God ! My God ! "

Rydal had held the gate open and a woman had entered after him. She came in almost furtively, hesitated, took in the house with a sweeping glance, then came forward with a defiant swagger :

" Well," she cried in a deep, penetrating voice, " you invited me. You made me come. On your own head be it ! There's a man, too, you said. I shall do better with the man."

Rydal advanced quickly and took her arm. " Go slow, Venetia. Go slow a bit at first."

She answered with anger at once wheedling and imperious. " What do you mean ? That I am not to have a drink ? "

" I wasn't talking about drink."

" You were. . . . About what, then ? "

He said nothing but turned to gaze into her face as he walked across the lawn beside her.

She was a woman still conspicuously beautiful, but the sag of ill-health had loosened the flesh of her cheeks, her eyes were heavy, their lashes greased together into little black curving sticks, their upper lids shiny ; her slim body was not fattened but it was blunted, its suppleness was gone ; there was a harsh glitter in the show of her teeth when she laughed. And now, at some thought within her, she laughed a thick, gusty laugh; then ceased, frightened, and there crept into her expression the absurd pathos of a clown denied his applause.

She and Henry came into the house. Carey did not move. Presently they came into the room.

" This is your mother, Carey. I have brought her home."

Mrs. Rydal would have kissed her, but Carey stood away and answered her father.

" What room is she to have ? "

" My own room, I suppose," Mrs. Rydal intervened. " Or is it yours now ? "

" No, it is not mine. It is empty. There is no furniture in it. I will have the bed made in the Pink Room. If you will come up with me, I will take you to my own room meanwhile."

Rydal introduced Richard and Mrs. Rydal gave him her hand.

" Did you, too, suppose that I was dead ? And even now, Carey stares at me as if she were seeing a ghost. What are we, Carey — friends or enemies ? "

Carey, pale and rigid, stood gazing, not at the newcomer but at her father, and Richard to comfort her said : " In any case, Carey, he is safe."

" Oh no," she answered, her eyes moving to her mother's face, " oh no, he is not safe."

PART THREE

" Say what you will, our God sees how they run.
These disillusions are His curious proving
That He loves humanity and will go on loving ;
Over there are faith, life, virtue in the sun."

EDMUND BLUNDEN

PART THREE

THAT July evening on which Henry Rydal brought his wife home might have been for all of them one of unrelieved tension and distress if a phrase spoken by Mrs. Rydal had not given Richard sudden hope. She opened her great eyes to a degree wilfully theatrical, stared at Carey over the dinner-table and said : "I must have been beautiful ! It's a pity I have gone to pieces." A narrow, deep wrinkle twitched at each corner of her mouth, and Henry put his hand for a moment on hers as if to thank her for this flicker of gaiety and generosity. She resented the touch and sulked in consequence, but her having spoken as she did suggested that the spark Henry had loved in her might not be altogether extinct.

There is salvation in the plain necessities of routine. The first intolerable encounter and recognition in the sitting-room before dinner had been spanned by the need of bringing in Mrs. Rydal's luggage from the car, of taking her to the Pink Room and providing for her there, of explaining to Mrs. Durrant who the visitor was and changing the order of the meal. These duties Carey had discharged with the courtesy of hostess to guest, but at dinner itself she was silent, and indeed what was there to speak of ? All her life she had believed that her mother was dead, imagining her as having died young in the flawless beauty of the portrait ; lately she had believed even that her father had been responsible for his wife's death ; and now this thickened and deteriorated woman, who was her mother, sat at table, and Carey did not know how she had come there, in what mood or under what compulsion or with what purpose her father had brought her. He had attempted no explanation other than : " Your mother was alone and ill, so I brought her here. You will look after her, Carey ? "

" Yes, Father."

But when dinner was over she could endure no more. Coffee was brought into the sitting-room ; she served it, then went out from the room and from the house. The gate creaked as she opened it.

" Where has the child gone ? "

" For a walk," Rydal answered.

Mrs. Rydal turned to Richard. " Does she normally go off for walks alone at this hour ? "

" No."

" What does she do ? "

" Settles down with us — here or in the garden."

" To do what ? I want to get an idea of how the house works."

" Sometimes I read aloud," Henry put in.

" I see. I have interrupted a reading. What was the book ? To read aloud was always your vanity, Henry."

" We enjoyed it in the old days."

" I hated it. I hated it. I was unutterably bored."

She had said this because it was untrue, because her pride's defence was to repudiate the past. In the same spirit, cruel, frightened, childishly defiant, she reached out for brandy and looked at Henry to watch the effect. If he protested, she would rage against him ; if he did not, she would despise him for not having dared to protest.

" What was the book ? " she persisted. Her eye fell on *Inglesant*. " This ? Was it this ? " She opened it, read, snapped it close. " Really, Henry ! That is what you are — you, the Sage, the unswerving lover — that is *all* you are : an intolerable sentimentalist, wallowing in the past ! "

Henry received this with a grace that was more than patience. " When you are unhappy, Venetia, you always attack. But to-morrow, when you wake up here, and sit by the stream——"

" With my memories of the past ! " she cried with scorn.

" No. With assurance of the future."

She shook her head. " With Carey, perhaps ?
I shall be back in London within a week. You know
that. I told you. You made me come. But I shall
go back again."

" No you won't."

" And who's to stop me ? Why shouldn't I go
back ? "

" Because in the end you will not want to." He
hesitated an instant before adding : " And because
you are ill."

She shrugged her shoulders and retorted with a
coarseness of tone intended to wound him : " Well,
we are quarrelling like a married couple — if nothing
else. Which is hard on Mr Cannock. Why didn't
you leave yourself in peace, Henry ? I have never
done you anything but harm. Why on earth did
you drag me back ? "

" Because I love you."

" Oh," she exclaimed, " I'm sick of the word.
I have heard it too often."

Soon after this the fighting strength went out of
her. She took more brandy, became very pale and
began to cry. Her crying was extraordinary, for she
made no attempt to conceal it. Upright in her chair,
her hands folded in her lap, she allowed her face to
pucker and her lips to tremble like a child's, and when
Henry held her in his arms she shook her head help-

lessly as if to say : it's of no use to try to comfort me ;
it goes deeper than that.

"Do not go, do not go ! " Henry said to Richard.
"Venetia is tired and ill, that is all. I will take her
to her room. Then I'll come back to you. We'll go
out and meet Carey."

On her way to the door, Mrs. Rydal stopped before
Richard and gave him her hand with perfect self-
command and with no trace in her manner of shame
or embarrassment.

"You endure a great deal. You must be fond of
Henry."

"I am."

"Then we have that in common. . . . Have you
any influence with Carey ? She is — in some ways —
like me. I expect you have."

"I had," Richard answered. "Now, I'm not
sure."

"Why has it changed ? "

"What ? "

"Your — influence with her ? Because of me ?
I don't understand."

"May we talk about it in the morning ? "

"No," she cried, "talk about it now. I can
stand. I can think. I'm not drunk." But she had
lost the thread of her questioning. "Are we very
alike ? Henry can't know. You see us from outside

— are we so alike, Carey and I ? "

" Almost——"

" Almost what — shockingly ?   Oh," she said, " you are thinking of our faces.   But it's more than that — much more.   Inside me, I am Carey.   No, I'm not.   I *was*."   Her self-control, her pride, her memory were slipping from her.   She opened her eyes wide, as she had at dinner.   " You see," she said slowly and comically, " poor Henry thinks he is going to reform me and make me into a good woman again——"

" I have never said or thought it," Rydal put in.

" I wanted him to deny it," she answered with a smile.   " Because, you see, it's quite, quite useless. Just a waste of time."   She threw up her head and compelled herself to speak clearly ; indeed, it was almost with Carey's own voice that she spoke then. " If I find that I am doing her harm, I will go away. I promise that.   I promise. . . . What a useless, silly promise !   The harm will be done."

From Henry Rydal, from Mrs. Seaton, and from Venetia herself, Richard learned the history of Henry's recent visits to London and of the distant past.

In France, during the holiday Venetia had shared with her husband twenty years ago, she had admitted as her lover a prosperous retailer named Rodney

Besting, who, while Henry was a prisoner of war, had steadily pursued her, vowing at each encounter that he respected her love for Henry and wished for nothing but to befriend and protect her. She had no natural taste for him, and, afterwards to Henry in England, had spoken of his persistence with her most active ridicule. He was fifty, blind and watery when he took off his thick glasses, shiny under his thinning hair; his pose was the paternal one, his professed ambition to hoist her on to his knee and prattle to her in baby-talk. Anyhow, she had said, he smells wrong.

Nevertheless, she had admitted that, in Henry's absence, she had used him. He had a prompt and executive mind. His car had been at her disposal in London, he had fed her and taken her to plays; he had flattered her sense of power and satisfied his own sense of generosity by giving jobs to her friends; when repairs were necessary at the Water House, he had reviewed the estimates and made the contracts. She told all this to Henry on his return from Germany, and had made no secret of it among her acquaintances. Besting had been an indiscreet joke. She called him her sugar-daddy or, alternatively, the Universal Provider, and damned him gently with faint praise, saying that his intentions were good, that for a tradesman he had a commendable " interest in art," that he had good teeth and wore expensive shirts.

Her and Henry's going to France together was to have been an end of Mr. Besting, but Mr. Besting thought otherwise. He had gone to Cannes to rediscover a woman he had known there in 1914, had observed grey hairs, and with one cheque had paid off her loyalty and his conscience ; then, hearing of the Rydals farther down the coast, had called. His visit was cleverly timed. A summons to a conference with lawyers in Paris had taken Henry away ; Venetia had been made angry by his going — his fault, in her eyes, had always been that he trusted her too well, was not jealous enough ; and she was correspondingly flattered by the appearance from Cannes of the good teeth, the expensive shirts, and by the persistence, now very thinly paternal, of what she called " the coral insect." She gave Besting his reward. Why ? Why now, after having so long despised him ? Experimentalism ? Perhaps because, in some obscurely contemptuous way, she was touched — as she contrasted it with Henry Rydal's exacting genius — by the man's abject hunger. Perhaps because, valuing Henry's judgment and taste more than any on earth, she was goaded, by his unconcealed scorn of Besting, into an extravagance of contradiction. " And in the end," she said, " it becomes boring to say no."

At that point, pride had entered in. Because she despised herself for what she had done and the man with whom she had done it, she told Rydal the truth and fiercely justified it. Actions are fluid, not binding, but words are prisons ; and Venetia threw in her lot with Mr. Besting because she talked herself into it and, in the end, was too weak to escape from him. To give dignity to the little shame by which she had intended nothing, to enable her to represent the sugar-daddy as a creditable figure, she had dramatized her pettiness, and said and said and said that he was a good man, devoted to her as Henry was not, and finally, in the desperation of one who slaps down on the table a ruinous stake, that she loved him. Having said so much, she had to find reasons for this grotesque affection. The Universal Provider waited, more pleased than embarrassed by her conflicting struggles to escape from him and to explain him. Each struggle to escape, each self-justifying reason she gave for its failure, was for him a welcome tightening of the chain.

Had he not, she exclaimed to Henry, for her sake and without at the time any promise from her, bought off the woman at Cannes ? Was he not prepared to bring financial pressure on his wife to release him ? Henry observed that money appeared to be Besting's convenient release from all his pledges. She replied that, on the contrary, he was so generous with money that he didn't mind what he paid to give her security and happiness. " He loves me ! " Venetia said. " He really loves me ! " Henry, she declared, was at once too romantic, too inhuman, too austere, too *proud* ! Very well, there was something in being even a coral insect ! That kind of persistence was a proof of love. And Rodney might not have either distinguished manners or distinguished conversation, but he didn't, like Henry, go away from her. He had real tenderness ! He had a pet name for her — and Henry had never had a pet name for her ! Rodney liked her to sit on his knee and be called " dear child." She was safe with him. There was nothing he would not do for her sake. She had taught him to put eau-de-Cologne behind his ears, and now he smelt better.

So she had gone, terrified, to the safety of her cage. Henry, for Carey's sake at first, had imposed upon himself the fiction that Venetia was dead, and had either sent to her or put out of sight everything that had belonged to her or was associated with her except the portrait, the piano and the wall-mirror above the fire-place in her bedroom. It had become for him a saving and necessary fiction, necessary to preserve uncorrupted the idea of love as he and she had known it, and, he believed, necessary to her in practice if she was to have any chance of building a tolerable existence with the Universal Provider. Mr. Besting, steadily beating down the allowances he had promised his wife on their separation, succeeded at last in driving that tired woman through the divorce court, married Venetia with the help of Henry's lawyers, and died. Henry did not hear of his death until several years afterwards. Venetia was reported to be living in Genoa under the name of Dipauli, and Helen Seaton's informant, through whom the news came, had added that Mrs. Dipauli wore bad jewellery and did not look after her hands. "It appeared," was Mrs. Seaton's comment to Richard when she reached this part of the narrative, "that the Universal Provider had failed to provide. Henry found out the Genoese address, but by that time she was gone — where no one knew — to Alexandria, as it turns out."

It was Henry Rydal himself who told Richard of the re-encounter in London, and he told it briefly.

"I had been in the London Library. I walked from Jermyn Street into Piccadilly by the passage that runs up at the side of the National Provincial. She was in a public telephone-box. I saw her through the glass door, fumbling in her bag for pennies, and she seemed not to have any. So I opened the door, handed in two pennies, shut the door and waited." Henry was delighted by the adventure. "You should have seen her face ! She came out of the box and kissed me. Odd, that was the first shock; it wasn't the same scent. Why, after twenty years, should one expect it to be the same scent?"

"It's true," Venetia said, commenting on this in her own version, "it's true I kissed him and he said at once: 'So you have come back!' I hadn't by any means. I kissed him because it was funny to see a hand come in through the door and give me two pennies. But to him it was — I suppose it was the kind of impulse he used to love in me, the kind that made him laugh, and he said: 'So you have come back!' as if the whole world had turned over. After that, it was a battle. He assumed that I should return here. I couldn't get it out of his head, so I took him to where I lived — not pretty — I told him about myself, I let him see, I made him see. Then, as a kind of joke, not a very good one, I said: 'But we are not even married any more. Had you forgotten that?' He answered — you know that smile of his that twitches the skin under his right eye? — he answered: 'Yes, completely.' It was true; he really had forgotten. 'Besides, we are,' he said. 'What we lawyers do or undo makes no odds. Your contract with the Universal Provider wasn't a marriage. Ours was and is. Marriage is an idea. Ideas live and are reborn; they go on. Nothing else does. The

Universal Provider was an account you opened at the Stores. Now it's paid and closed. He's deader than dead.' "

She repeated Henry's words with fascinated and painful accuracy — the very words unquestionably, for his intonation was in her way of repeating them ; then, after a pause, added slowly : " I hated him for that ! All over again I hated him for that ! "

" Why ? " Richard asked. " It's his whole doctrine. Facts aren't important in themselves. They exist only in relation to ideas."

" I know, I know," she said, " it wasn't that. I believe that too. If I didn't, it would seem wrong that you should call me ' Mrs. Rydal,' which isn't legally my name, but it seems natural that you should ; I think of myself in that way. Oh, yes," she continued, " in that I believe what Henry believes. That's why I ever loved him, and why, inside me, I *am* Carey. Do you understand ? "

" But not why you ' hated ' him for saying it ! "

" I tell you it wasn't that ! " she exclaimed angrily. " It was his contempt for — for the Universal Provider. I should never have gone to — to Mr. Besting if Henry hadn't despised him. And, after all," she said reflectively, " he wasn't a bad man. He always promised more than he could perform, but that's a habit of tradesmen hungry for business. And it's true he was a bore in company — pompous and skittish at the same time, and he had the kind of accent that isn't quite bad enough to be laughed off as a joke. But alone, when I hadn't got to be ashamed of him, he was rather comfortable, like a very attentive butler when you are ill. Anyhow, whatever he was, it was I who had to live with him, and to say, after twenty years, that he was an account I opened at the Stores wasn't a credit to me."

After twenty years, they had again quarrelled bitterly on the subject of Mr. Besting, she in her perpetual need of self-justification, Henry unable to accept that her defence of him sprang now, as in the past, from this need and from her knowledge, of all knowledge the hardest to bear, that her notions of domesticity with Mr. Besting had made her ridiculous.

In France, Henry had let her go ; in London he returned to battle day after day, sought her in her lodging and in the streets, undeterred by her violence, her abuse, her drink, her paraded squalors, undiverted now — for at last he had perceived the trick she was playing on herself — even by the stories she could not resist telling of Besting, Dipauli, their successors and assigns. She was ill physically and, he believed, in peril of becoming ill mentally ; he was determined to bring her home. His most formidable obstacle was her pride — she didn't want his pity, she wasn't a refugee, above all she would not challenge what she assumed must be the enmity of her own daughter. He swore to her that in assuming Carey's enmity she was wrong. " And how do you know ? Have you told her about me ? Have you said you have met me ? Of course not. You don't dare ! " But he had kept his head. To have told Carey would, he knew, have prompted in Venetia the retort that he had " asked permission." Instead he had answered : " No, my dear, I haven't told her and shall not. She believes you dead and so she may, unless you have the courage to come."

Courage ! Was it that challenge which in the end had brought her ? Or poverty, sickness, fear, a desire to be looked after ? " I believe," said Helen Seaton, " that what brought her was curiosity as much as anything else — and curiosity, in Venetia, isn't altogether a vice. She has always loved to put a new frame round her picture of herself and see what she looks like. It isn't a vice, and scarcely, if you'll believe me, vanity in the ordinary sense. She doesn't by any means necessarily *admire* the picture. But except when she duped herself over Besting and went about pretending she was a baby to be eternally dandled on that lamentable knee, she has always known that her good lies in freedom — freedom even from a too fixed, a too rigid individuality — and the whole point of Henry is that he everlastingly re-imagines a woman he loves ; it's his way of loving her ; he isn't the kind of fool who ties a woman down to one set of facts."

" And Besting ? "

" I am not sure," she answered. " I saw little of him. I don't think he was evil. Sentimental and stubborn, chiefly. He had an awkward habit of whining — of saying that he was ill or lonely and trading on pity to get what he wanted. And if ever Venetia crossed him in some trifle, if she was late for example, he became ' hurt,' like a bad school-master when he is ragged. But still, I don't think he was bad. Just badly brought up. He might have been all right," Mrs. Seaton added thoughtfully, " if he had been allowed to play with dolls."

Richard asked what on earth she meant.

" Well," she replied, " he treated human beings like that. Nice to pat and spoil for a bit as long as they were acquiescent ; if not — away with them into a cupboard. And I expect he *was* lonely. None of his women stayed with him long, I gather, and certainly he seemed not to have a man friend in the world, apart from a few toadies among those he employed. He explained that by saying he hadn't had ' the advantages of a University acquaintance.' Indeed, he hadn't, but still, you'd think a man would pick up a friend somewhere in fifty years."

But Richard was already aware that Helen Seaton's analysis of the human animal was too neatly compartmental. Like a general who accurately estimates a military position without noticing the revolution that shall make nonsense of it, she judged men by their conduct and interest, making no allowance for imaginative overtones. Probably Besting had had qualities of painstaking kindliness for which she awarded him less than his due. Her judgment of humanity was based almost too sharply on the visible, the social evidence. Certainly, to her, the likeness between Venetia and Carey was "a remarkable physical resemblance"—no more; and Richard preferred for wisdom the comment made by Flower when, having gone to the Water House and for the third time seen mother and daughter together, he returned to the laboratory. "I don't much care for it, Mr. Cannock: I will say that. Like two opposite mirrors, reflecting each other. If they go on looking, they'll go mad."

When Venetia had been nearly three weeks at Sarley Down, Richard came home one evening to find house and garden empty. Henry and Venetia had, he supposed, gone down to the brook, but Carey would not have gone with them. He climbed the stairs and started towards his bedroom, intending to read there. On the way he passed the door, which was standing open, of the room, above the dining-room, that had formerly been empty. The walls had been re-whitewashed, a carpet laid, curtains re-hung. In the last few days furniture had been moved in. Now it was almost ready for Venetia to occupy, and Richard, remembering it as it had been and the figure that had appeared at its window, went in to look at it.

Carey, with her back to him, was standing on a low stool adjusting the curtains of a four-poster. With arms still upraised and body taut, she turned her head and looked down at him, the thought that had been hers before his arrival continuous in her eyes, and in the instant during which this thought over-lapped her recognition of him, he saw, as if he had been admitted below the surface even of her own consciousness, that she had proceeded beyond un-happiness, far beyond personal jealousy, resentment or fear, and was in spiritual peril. He had seen the same invaded look twice before : in a young soldier who had maimed himself ; in a girl who had stood near him in the cathedral of Sens, and kneeled, and risen again unable to pray, and gone out.

He asked her to leave her task and come out with him.

" I have finished it," she said.

" Then come."

" Not to the brook."

He suggested that they should go through the east meadows, across the railway and back through Findon wood. She answered " yes," came down from the stool and went with him out of the house, bareheaded, delaying for nothing.

" Don't be kind to me," she said. " It's no good, Richard. I know you have wanted to talk to me. That's why I came — for the sake, I suppose, of what there might have been between us — at least of what I thought there might have been : I can say it now."

" It's you I want to do the talking, Carey."

She answered doubtfully : " Something has dried up in me."

" Why ? "

" Ah, I wish I knew ! "

" But you haven't been hostile to her. You have done everything on earth for her that you humanly could do."

" Oh yes," she replied, " I have had her room whitewashed and have hung the curtains. I have *done* everything. Doing is no good."

They walked for a long time in silence through the warm, quiet air.

" What is it you are afraid of ? Not of her ? "

She was grateful for so much understanding. " Of myself," she replied. " I wonder whether I can tell you. Helen Seaton thinks I am jealous of Venetia's coming into what was *my* house or that I can't endure Father's love for her. It's not that. If it were, everything would be simple : either she could go away or I, and we have discussed that ; there's a dreadful, cold sanity between us sometimes, and we have discussed it and it's no good. If she died, it would be no good. She and I are locked together. I suppose I have been arrogant without knowing it," Carey continued. " I have just begun to understand that. I loved Father and I loved you, Richard, and I thought that what Father calls ' the principle of love ' — the power to love *through* criticism, to recognize vileness but not to be dried up by it — was in me. That was my peace of mind. Nothing could touch it. It was the peace of God in me — so I believed. Now I know that it was utterly false — a much deeper lie than any she has lied to herself. I was a prig, that's all — an odd kind of prig ; and she is a frightened egoist. She pretends to be brave, not to be afraid of life, and she lashes out at it like an animal at bay, then runs for shelter — Mr. Besting's, Father's, anyone's. She so hates herself that she will fawn on anyone who will dramatize her." Carey broke off in terror, listening to the echo in her mind of what she had just said. " I say that ! I think that ! I know that superficially it is true. But I know it is not true of any human being. To think it, is to hate. And if I hate, there's nothing left of me." She had been speaking gently, but now again the wave of her mother's influence flowed over her and she spoke with her mother's passionate irony. " Venetia says that all she has ever wanted is security and peace and a home, and yet, wherever she is, there is tension. She struggles to create it, like a decaying actress who overplays and overplays the old tricks — anything to keep an audience. Oh, Richard," Carey said, halting in the wood and looking up at him, " why do I say that ? I can't help it. The thought comes, the words come, as if she inhabited me. I can't love any more — neither Father nor you nor anyone. It is my own bitter, wicked fault."

Her eyes were wide and bright, her lips parted, and her hair, through which she had been running her hand, stood up from the forehead and away from the temples in great pluming curves. This startled wildness accented her youth, and Richard, seeing her first as a child frightened in this branched and leafy sunlight, saw her in the next instant as a woman he desired and loved, in whose peace his own resided, in whose agonized confusion the summing of his own life was confused ; but he made no movement towards her ; it was as if she were walking in her sleep, inhabitant of a world into which he might not violently enter. He dared no more than to take her hand and continue to hold it as they walked, and for this she seemed grateful. She turned her head to look at him, and her cold fingers moved in his when he said : " Look at it this way, Carey. In one aspect all our lives — your father's, mine, now your own, even the life of a people — consist in being invaded by ghosts. And the ghosts we fear are the familiar ones, from which our own eyes look out at us. We can't hate them without hating ourselves. We can never destroy them."

" Did Father ever speak to you of ghosts ? "

" Never. Why ? "

" Only that, when I was a child, I slept in the dressing-room opposite the room you found me in just now. Its being without furniture made it different from any other room I had known, and I used to imagine there was someone in it. One night I woke suddenly, certain of it. I wasn't frightened. I was interested. I went along the passage to look. You remember, the one thing there has always been in that room was a gilt mirror. The wire was long, the mirror leaned out from the wall, and when I looked up I saw my face and the shoulders of my night-dress and my candle ; it was exciting, I don't know why. I stood still and stared ; I thought that whoever was in the room would appear over my shoulder. It was

Father who came. He picked me up, asked what I was doing there. I said, quite cheerfully I think, that I was 'looking for the ghost.' He carried me out ; he thought I was frightened and took me into his own bed. We sat there, his arm round me, and sang my songs, and he read me the story of Gehazi. Then it struck me as odd that we should be singing our songs at that time of night, and I said : ' Why are we singing our songs ? ' ' To lay the ghost,' he said. I asked what did it mean — to *lay* a ghost ? He said ' to give it rest.' I said : ' But how ? By singing songs ? ' He answered : ' Yes, singing songs was one way,' and, when I asked what other ways there were, he tightened his arm round me and said : ' I'm not sure, Carey. By love, I think.' ''

When she had done, Carey said : '' What made me begin to tell that story ? I have never told it before.''

In telling it she had come so far and so happily away from the cause of her division of mind that Richard shrank from the cruelty of recalling her to it ; nevertheless, he said deliberately : '' We were talking of your mother.''

'' I remember.''

'' I think, in a sense, she has always been here, Carey.''

She astonished him by saying calmly : '' I know

that." Then, turning aside from the impulse of compassion which, he had believed, might have prevailed in her if she could but have imagined her mother's suffering, she said with a compelled and tormented hardening of her heart : " I thought she was dead. It's easy enough to idealize those who are dead."

From her four-poster, which stood out from the corner of her room, Venetia could see the top of the wall that enclosed the lawn, and, beyond the wall, the farm buildings opposite and the church. It was a scene that had held place in her memory through all the years of her absence ; she had imagined herself in this room, moving about it, going to the window to look out ; in Italy, in Egypt, in London, she had watched the light change on the elms beyond the farm and the flapping of rooks, and heard the farm noises and the church bell.

This bell was reserved now as the tocsin of invasion, but the clock had struck six and the end of organ music from within the church told that the evening service was begun. Carey and Richard Cannock were, she knew, attending it, Henry was in his library below, and she sat on her bed, more profoundly lonely than she had ever been in the long bitterness of her travels. During them the idea of this home and of her days of happiness in it had remained a living idea. She had not believed that she would ever in the flesh re-enter it but the idea of it had been the core of her idea of herself. Come what might, she had been Henry's wife, had loved him, had borne his child, had lived well and innocently in this place ; and she had had, in all her griefs and follies, the innermost assurance that she was *that* woman, neither corrupt nor heartless nor mercenary, not within herself the acquisitive and sentimental doll that she had become for Besting's pleasure. Now she had been brought home. Henry was unswervingly patient ; he loved her still but his love only surprised her, she had lost the power to respond to it ; she fell into rages of scorn against his gentleness, against the quiet routine of the house, against everything she wished to love. Her relationship with Carey was frozen ; the idea that had for so long been the flower of her consolation was choked by this barren reality. Henry had believed, not indeed that she would be " reformed " or grow young again, but that from the reality, if they faced it together, there would spring a new flowering of the idea. This had not been so. She had blamed Carey for the failure ; with all the fierceness of her irony she had attacked Henry's vain idealism ; now most bitterly she blamed herself : I have no heart, I am incapable of love — of giving or receiving it. I ought not to have come.

This she had said to Henry and had asked him to consent to her going away, but she had known, as she made the request, that it was meaningless ; he would not consent and indeed could not — she was too ill. While she was in London, before he discovered her, she had in fact faced her illness alone ; for many days it would leave her free, then there would be pain in her foot and in the upper part of her nose ; it would spread across her left brow, and grip her head, and at the same time her strength, even her will, would go from her. She felt she was rotting. When the pain slackened a period of physical exhaustion would succeed it in which she would lie on her bed or in a chair without clear recognition of her own identity or need of food or drink. From such an attack, the third since her coming from London, she was now recovering. This Sunday she had been about the house again and had walked as far as the brook. After tea she had come to her room to rest, wishing to please Henry by appearance at supper.

Now the wish to be gay at supper crept into her mind. Whatever else might have failed in her, she could still be brilliant and challenging company when in a good mood ; Henry would praise her for it and she loved to be praised. She walked to the window and looked down. A white hen, belonging to the farm, had come into the garden and, having forgotten the way out, was fretting on the lawn in little runs and pauses and peckings, unable to remember for long what she was looking for ; and Venetia, amused by the hen, began vaguely to think that, when she turned away from the window and crossed the room towards the cupboard in which was hanging the dress she proposed to wear, she would, on the way, pass the bookcase. It was glass-fronted and locked, the key was in a vase on the mantelpiece.

The thought of bookcase and key slid across her mind like a face in the window of a passing train, casual and irrelevant, for she had no intention of opening the bookcase or of taking from their shelf the section of books that began on the left with *The Tenant of Wildfell Hall* and ended on the right with *The Greek Commonwealth* ; nevertheless she knew that by a firm inward pressure of her hands she could lift out in one piece the section of nine volumes and, if there should be need, return it swiftly to its place. The hen, retreating from the desert of unfamiliar lawn, had taken cover under a rhododendron bush, and Venetia decided to go down and show her the way back to her own people in the farmyard opposite. First she would change her dress for the dress in the cupboard. When she lifted the vase from the mantel-piece the key chinked in it and turned out easily into her palm. There were people of whom it could truly

be said that they drank ; their craving was supposed
to be irresistible — a thing she had never been able
fully to understand ; nothing was irresistible ; if you
felt that danger approaching, it would be easy enough
to say : no more except after dinner with coffee or
none except on Saturday evenings or, clearly and
definitely, none at all. But to make rules of that
kind was an admission of weakness. In her they were
unnecessary for she had complete control of herself
and could do without brandy at any time. The only
reason for her keeping a bottle concealed behind the
books was that Henry had a fear of her drinking
brandy and — just because he was so gentle about it
and did not preach or blame her — she thought it
better, when she did need a glass at other times than
after dinner, not to distress him by taking it in his
presence. Besides there was, in her case, no danger
in the secrecy. She had no craving that she could
not resist. Now, for instance, if she wanted to, she
could drop the key again into the vase and put the
thought of brandy out of her mind while changing her
dress.

Of course it is true, she thought as she unlocked
the bookcase and felt, with the joy there always is in
precise repetitions, the weight of the nine volumes
that came out so neatly between her hands — of
course it is true that, when Besting began to plod

after me, I had no craving for anything he could offer and laughed at the notion of his obtaining power over me, and brandy may be, like him, "a coral insect"; after to-day I will run no risks; I will not keep a bottle here any more. It was delightful to her to think, as she poured the liquid into a medicine glass, that her resolution was taken, that she was safe — for after all she had been a little frightened — and that what she was doing was being done for the last time. She felt better when she had swallowed, and at the second glass she thought that this evening at supper she would be happy and gay; everyone would laugh, and afterwards in the garden she would tell stories and read verses — once Carey had said she read verses beautifully. The difficulty was to know what to do with the bottle if she was no longer to keep it here. If she put it in the cupboard downstairs with brandy still in it, it would be noticed, and to empty the brandy away, to waste it as if she were afraid of it, would be absurd. She observed then how little remained. If she drank it, to get rid of the empty bottle would be easy.

There was a knock on the door. She remembered with a pang which struck like a knife in her left arm and side that she had forgotten to lock it, but she had the presence of mind to cry out "One moment!" and, with agility that made her laugh inwardly, put in the cork, laid the bottle down on the shelf, lifted in the section of books, and closed the glass doors.

" Come in ! . . . You, Henry ! Have you finished your work ? "

" Yes. Packed up for the day. How are you, my dear ? "

She smiled and said she was feeling much better.

" I thought," Henry said, " that you might like to come down into the garden. They will be in from church soon. This is the perfect moment to drink sherry — cool sherry in a deck-chair on a warm summer's evening."

" I'll come out," she said. " I should like that. But I don't want any sherry."

As she spoke, Henry, near the bookcase, drew away from it and looked at his own hand which had been on the ledge at the base of the glass doors, and she saw that the brandy was trickling under the books, under the doors, over the ledge, and falling in a little stream on to the carpet.

She said with the loudness of panic : " I think, when I have had one of my attacks, it's always best to drink nothing except perhaps a little claret at dinner."

Henry put his arm round her shoulder. " Come down into the garden when you are ready. I'll wait for you there."

A devil in her prevented her from accepting the avoidance he offered.

"Why aren't you angry with me?" she said. "Why don't you punish me? Yes, that is brandy all over the floor! If you had punished me, I should never have gone to Besting — do you know that?"

Henry smiled and held her shoulder. "Very well," he said. "I had thought it tactful to leave you to mop it up. But if not — not. Let it drip. Now do what you are told and come out."

She said: "You're good to me, Henry. But you are a fool."

"I love you. Is that why I'm a fool?"

"I think so," she answered. "I'm not lovable."

"Everyone thinks that who is afraid of themselves."

She shook her head. "I don't know what that means"; then turned away to the fireplace: "I think *now* I love you. Anyhow I can say so — even to myself. You have more power of imagination in you than anyone I have ever known. This was an empty room and you have filled it."

She was watching herself play the scene; he knew the mood, caught the intonation, loved her well enough to discount them.

"Then come out," he said.

At that her practical sense of humour jolted her into action.

" Very well. Go on. I'll follow. There are the servants to think of. I'll clear this up."

Her back was towards him, but, as he reached the door, she turned and faced him and said :

" It's no good, Henry. I'm hopeless. I can't ever come to life again. You think I can, but I can't, and you can't make me."

" You are more alive," he answered, " than anyone I have ever known."

" That's because you imagine."

" Well, it may be. It's none the less real. You said this room was empty — and now ? "

She said quietly : " What is your word — the Greek Kalends ? . . . When they come, perhaps I shall stop betraying myself."

" What would help you most, Venetia ? "

For a long time she was silent. " Carey."

" I know."

" She was a baby when I went away. It's as if I had killed her then, and now I am killing her again. Listen, Henry. I am talking sense now. When you have gone out of the room, I don't know, perhaps I shall hate you for knowing about the brandy, and to-night at supper God knows what I shall say. Cruel things, perhaps. My tongue says them. I can't help it. But now I'm sane enough. And it's not just an empty threat — I shall go from here. The thing has failed. We may as well recognize it. Nothing can save it."

"One thing can," he answered. "You call it imagination, but you speak of it as if it were fancy or hypnotism or witchcraft. It isn't, you know. Imagination consists in seeing things as they are — as they really are, their essences, not as they appear to be. It is the supreme realism of the spirit. The paradox is that love is its cause *and* its effect. I have it towards you ; that is why I love you and how I love you. And if Carey——"

Venetia shook her head. "Carey love me ?"

"Not what you appear to be. What you are."

"Henry — dear, dear Henry — isn't that just words ? The hard-boiled people would say so, and they are in a fair way towards ruling the world."

"Towards appearing to rule the appearances of the world," he answered. "They have never yet succeeded in doing more than that. What they crucify always rises from the dead."

It was not long after this that Venetia, who seldom proceeded by frontal attack, surprised Richard by saying : "Tell me something. It would help me. There is a thing I must decide for myself, but if you could give me a straight answer to one question it would help me to decide. What is happening between you and Carey ? "

" A deadlock."

" Why ? You love her ? "

" Yes."

" And she you ? Helen Seaton told me so."

" You have discussed us with Mrs. Seaton ? Well," Richard said, " I suppose it's natural. What was her view ? She always has one, cut and dried. She is the most definite woman I have ever known. She knows the reasons for everything. She has a mind like a memorandum from the Ministry of Economic Warfare. Why, according to her, are Carey and I at a deadlock ? "

He said this with a sceptical smile that roused Venetia to Helen Seaton's defence. " She isn't the fool you suppose."

" I don't suppose anything of the kind. She is very far from being a fool. That is why I asked for her opinion."

" She said," Venetia replied, " that you were losing Carey because you didn't propose."

" That is definite enough ! "

" Is it untrue ? "

" Listen," he answered. " If you see someone you love sleep-walking on the edge of a precipice, do you shout at them about your own affairs ? "

Venetia accepted this. " Very well. Forget Helen Seaton. You have put into words the question I wanted to ask you — why is Carey ' sleep-walking on the edge of a precipice ' ? "

" I wish," he said, " you would answer that your-self. If either you or she could answer it, Carey would wake and the precipice cease to exist. All I know — all I can say — is from outside. I am like the fool in an audience who shouts to warn the players on a stage against the danger he sees approaching them. They can hear him with their ears, but it makes no odds ; they don't hear him, they can't hear him, in the life that he is watching ; they have to feel the danger themselves."

" I suppose," Venetia said, " that the answer is simple enough — she hates me."

" Do you believe that ? "

" Sometimes I don't. Sometimes, Richard, I feel as if I *were* Carey. That will seem wicked and false to you. How can anyone who has lived as I have feel that ? And perhaps it's a lie. I don't know any longer what is false and what is true in me — when I am dramatizing myself and when I'm not. But I know that Carey is afraid and that because she's afraid she is frozen. I have been through that myself. I went through it when I was young and I am still going through it. What I am afraid of is — is the only hopeless, desperate sin : hardness of heart."

" So is she." Richard said.

" So is she," Venetia assented. " I know. That is the deadlock between her and me. I suppose another way of putting it is : I need her forgiveness " — Venetia smiled suddenly — " and how I should hate to be forgiven ! "

" ' Forgiven — forgiveness ' ! " Richard answered. " No one, in that sense, the sense of being patronized, of hearing a friend say : ' You were wrong, I am noble enough to put it out of my mind ' — no one, in that sense, wants to be forgiven — only to be re-imagined. That's what, as yet, she is incapable of. So are you towards her, Venetia. You are still thinking of her as your child."

She sighed. " Is anyone capable of it ? "

" Henry."

" Ah, but he loves me ! "

" So we come full-circle."

She searched his face, trying to understand ; then, in a flash, understood. " The cause *and* the effect ? " she said.

He repeated her words, asked what they meant.

" It was only something Henry said to me," she replied, and added slowly : " Thank you, Richard. You have at any rate given me what I wanted — a decision."

" And it is ? "

" To take myself off.   To go."

" You mean — to desert him a second time ? "

" ' Desert ' ? " she echoed.   " Is that the word ?
I think not.   I have often wondered whether you
have in the least understood how Henry and I parted ?
Or in what way we loved each other and still love
each other ?   You must remember, it was not only
that I went away ; it was that, when he might have
held me, he let me go."

" I myself have wondered what you were,"
Richard answered.   " You have said often that you
are Carey."

" You feel that is nonsense ? "

" No.   The odd thing is I feel it to be true."

" Beyond the physical likeness ? "

" Apart from it.   There is such a thing as the effect
of an individuality, altogether apart from things seen
and words spoken, just as handwriting has an effect,
a special humanity, that has nothing to do with the
words written ; and again and again, when you have
been behind me in a room or have come into the
garden without my seeing you, I have felt that it was
Carey who was there."

Venetia smiled at this.   " That was what Henry
loved in me — what you have found in Carey.   He
used to say I was ' absolute ' — which didn't mean

that I was perfect, or that I was honest or trust-worthy — though I was, or that he could in fact rely on my keeping my word. It wasn't by any means that we 'took each other for granted.' It was that somehow — perhaps because loving him wasn't a separate or a new thing with me but a part of love — somehow I let him know that he and I hadn't to go on guessing from year to year but that already the whole of our lives were one, the future and the past. There was no thought that one of us might betray the other ; I think we knew that, even if we did, it would make no difference ; we would still be one ; and whoever came between us, no one would matter in the end, no one would break us into two."

"Then why——" Richard began.

"Why did I go ? Or why did he let me ? "

"Is there one answer to both questions ? "

"There is no answer to either — except that I didn't believe I was going or he that I was gone. If you ask why I chose the other man — why in the first instance, I mean — the answer is that I didn't *choose* him. I went to bed with him. It was to have been for me a thing that was done and over. Just because I loved Henry and should always love him, it gave me pleasure to think that *once* there had been a man not Henry. Do you understand that ? It is an explanation, not an excuse. It has always amused me to put on another woman's dress; it was the same impulse — as trivial. Except that Besting had taken a lot of trouble about me and I liked him for that, he was anonymous. And then I told Henry. It wasn't the luxury of confession. It wasn't to salve my conscience. I hadn't even a feeling of guilt. I told him —" She was silent, struggling for the truth. "I told him because words are alive for me. Have you ever written a letter with no intention of sending it and sealed it with no intention of sending it, and walked out with it — still meaning not to send it; and then heard it drop into the letter-box? After that," she added, "everything followed, words followed, like wedges, driven in by little taps of blame and defence and mistrust and lying. We knew what was happening. Once we sat down together and said: We're losing each other. We love each other. We are losing each other. Let's talk it out and get it straight. But we couldn't. Words. Besting's name. I had to justify him. Henry had to speak of him as if— I remember now. The words, clearly. Henry and I had gone down to the shore. We could say more quietly there what we had to say. Even then neither of us believed that we were lost. I talked about marriage with Besting because I didn't in my heart believe in it. I said it would happen, but I didn't *see* it happening to me. I told him that Besting was not what he supposed but genuinely wished to marry me. ' He will conform,' Henry said. I knew there was something behind his choice of that word. It had a special meaning for us, a special scornful bitterness, but I couldn't think what, and, like a fool, I asked. ' Conform ? ' I said. And like a fool Henry asked whether I had forgotten the verses of Hardy called ' The Conformers ' that we had often read together. He didn't believe I had forgotten. He thought I was lying or afraid. He repeated them. ' You and Besting,' he said, ' a pretty marriage — you can recite Hardy to him at breakfast.

> ' We shall not go in stealth
> To rendezvous unknown,
> But friends will ask me of your health,
> And you about my own.
> When we abide alone,
> No leapings each to each,
> But syllables in frigid tone
> Of household speech.'

Words. Words, on and on, that neither of us intended. Those who love should be often silent." She lifted her head and shook it to break the web of that mis-understanding. "We didn't *part*," she said. "We spoke words to each other across the darkness, and when we stretched out our hands we missed, we couldn't find each other's hands again."

" But now ? " Richard asked.

" Ah, no ! Ah, no ! " she replied. " Did you seriously ask that ? Sometimes we are very near, Henry and I. But we shall never, never touch while Carey is between us. We shall always be one, he and I. We always have been. But it is possible for two people to be one without being able to touch. Then they are better apart while they live. Afterwards, perhaps, it may be different."

She took his hand as Carey would sometimes take it and said : " Try to remember this talk with me. When people kill themselves for clear and good reasons, the coroner's jury always adds the stupid insult that they killed themselves while of unsound mind. I shall not kill myself. I am still too greedy for life, such as it is. But I shall go. And when I am gone, don't let them say I was mad or hysterical, and don't let Henry follow me. I know quite clearly what I am doing and why. And don't put up the ridiculous story of a mother's heroic self-sacrifice for her child. It is true that I have begun to see her as something else than that — to ' re-imagine ' her, perhaps. I'm not evil and I'm not a fool. But what I do will be done quite deliberately — as much for my sake as for hers."

The impulse to argue with her was strong — to say : do not run away ; it would do no good ; to run away now would be the last betrayal ! As one never believes a man who says that he will kill himself, so Richard did not believe that Venetia's intention to go was firm, and he did not wish, by dispute, to crystallize it. Never attempt to argue a self-dramatizing woman out of the part she is playing. To her, argument is an equivalent of applause. Wait until she tires of it. And all he would allow himself to say was :

" But remember — you won't empty the room by going from it."

" For Henry ? "

He drew a bow at a venture : " Or for yourself."

" Ah ! " she exclaimed, " that is cruel ! What do you know ? Why should you say that ? "

She had, as she spoke to Richard, genuinely intended to leave the Water House. How, she did not know. Suddenly, without farewells — certainly ; but how ? by train ? by car ? — she had no plan. What possessions she had must be left behind. She must disappear finally, leaving no address. That night she counted the money in her purse — four pounds, three florins, a sixpence, a note for a hundred French francs now presumably valueless — and was glad to find there was so little ; it lent to her going a desperateness, an excitement, that reinforced her courage. Next day and the next, she began to take her farewells of the house. Everything she did was for the last time — or almost the last. She went into Henry's library while he was working — a thing she knew he liked as long as she didn't speak to him — and took down from the shelves book after book for the strange pleasure and agony of reflecting that now she would never read them and that, as she returned each to its place, she had touched it for the last time. To-morrow, she thought, I shall get up as soon as it is light and walk to the station. I will take my dispatch-case only, anything else would be too heavy, and buy a ticket for — for Cambridge perhaps, but leave the train at an earlier station — Henry will not know where.

But to vanish in war-time was not easy. She would have to take her ration card, and her heart failed at the thought that somehow she must steal it from Mrs. Durrant. First, she must find out where it was kept; even then, she did not know how many pages, how many coupons, Mrs. Durrant might have deposited with the local tradesmen; she did not understand pages and coupons; the difficulty of doing what she intended to do entangled her will; and suddenly she looked at Henry's shoulders, bowed over his desk, and smiled a long, deep, secret smile, thinking : if the Universal Provider were here, he would say, " Leave it to me, dear child. I will send my

Rolls-Royce. I will make all arrangements for your journey." But the Universal Provider was in his urn. She put her arm across Henry's shoulder, and laid her face against his and kissed him. It was the first time, since her return, that she had, on her own initiative, kissed him; she remembered that, if she was going to-morrow morning, it would be the last; tears came into her eyes; she dragged herself away and returned to her chair by the bookshelves. If this was her last day, she would at least not interrupt his work by an emotional scene.

He said: "Bless you, Venetia. I wanted that," and she heard his pen move on the paper and the little shift now and then of his body in his chair as she had heard them when he, returned from imprisonment in Germany, had said: now we can do the work we want to do. Then, while he spoke, Besting had been in her mind, but she had told Henry what there was to tell and had feared nothing. She and Henry had been together again, their marriage the exceptional marriage that was a partnership also, never to be broken in act or spirit; she had believed that, when they returned from their holiday in France, they would settle again here, this would be their home always, though they might have to spend time in London as long as he was in active practice at the Bar, and here, she had thought, with Carey, her baby, and perhaps a son, she would grow old happily.

Now, with a fierce wrench of her mind, she tried to mock the sentimentality of this remembrance, but could not. She thought of herself alone to-morrow afternoon — she would be there by lunch-time — at some inn near Cambridge. How would she spend the afternoon? Unpacking — but there would be nothing to unpack. She would sit and wait, and talk to the innkeeper, and count her money, which would by then be less than four pounds. Even when she returned to London, she could not go to her old lodging with Mrs. Gedge, for Henry would find her there. There was a man named Phillerby who ran a correspondence school of commercial art and had said that if ever she needed a job — but that had been months ago; she had his address, but were there any longer correspondence schools of commercial art? Since the war began, the whole world had changed its address. Except Rydal, the Water House, Sarley Down.

She had travelled so far in her thoughts — had, indeed, imagined herself in an underground railway near Euston, remembering this house, projecting herself into it — that the movement of the pen and the sound of a mowing-machine from the lawn filled her by their reality with an intolerable sense of the unreality of all else. She could not again go into exile. It would be better to die. In her bedroom were eleven half-grains of morphia that a young doctor, whose name she did not know, had given her as payment in kind. Twice before she had tried to use them and failed. Now she knew certainly that she would not fail. She would take them to-night in her own room. Afterwards, would Henry take out the furniture and empty the room ?

" Venetia," he said, " will you marry me ? " He turned in his chair. " Why don't you answer ? It is one of the questions that it is polite to——"

His tone, smiling and gentle, changed as he saw her face. She shook her head and answered : " I will go. I shall spoil your morning's work," and rose to go out. At the door she said : " Why did you ask that now ? "

" You kissed me of your own accord."

" Oh," she answered, " I can do that ! Look — I can do it again ! "

He put out his arms to hold her, but she stood back, having kissed him.

" Venetia, you love me. Is it true ? "

" Yes," she said, " at this moment it is true. At this moment, I love you with all my heart."

" Then where are you going ? "

" Into the garden."

"If you go, I shall go with you."

"Oh no! Oh no!" she cried. "You can't do that. Stay and go on with your work or I shall blame myself."

Still he would have come. When she saw this, she became suddenly angry, and, thinking of the young doctor who had given her the morphia, she cried out: "I don't want to be touched!"

She went to her bedroom to make sure that the morphia had not been mislaid; then sat down in a chair by the window overlooking the lawn and felt the room about her.

Richard had never known Venetia as gentle and calm as she was that evening at dinner. She talked easily and without self-assertion or extravagance. Carey said to him as they came from the dining-room: "She is different to-night — as though something inside her had decided itself. What has happened?"

Her father overheard the question and said: "She was like that, Carey, when she was young."

Venetia had gone ahead into the sitting-room. After they had been there a little while, she said to Carey: "Will you do something for me? Bring me *John Inglesant*."

"It is here," Carey answered. "At least it ought to be. We had it in this room."

"No. It has been put back. It is in the library, behind the writing chair, on the left, the fourth shelf from the bottom. I saw it there this morning."

"I will bring it," Richard said.

"No. I want Carey to bring it if she will. I want only her hands to touch it."

"What is it?" Henry asked with a smile. "A sorcery?"

"What do you call it?" Venetia replied. "There is a Latin name for it. What do you call it when you open a book by chance and seek an omen in it?"

Carey returned with the book and offered it to her mother, but Venetia did not take it.

"You open it, Carey."

"Where?"

"Anywhere."

"And give it to Father to read?"

"No. Will you read it yourself? Come and sit beside me to read."

Carey hesitated; almost she went; but, with the implied excuse that Venetia should not be troubled to make a place for her on the sofa, sank down in mid-floor, her feet drawn under her, and, with a smile of pretended mystery as though she were playing her part in a game, began to read:

" ' " I should prefer to say," replied the Spaniard,— and as he spoke his expression was wonderfully compassionate and urbane,—" I should prefer to say that there are some men whom God is determined to win by love." ' "

" Stop a moment, Carey," her father said, and it was not until her face had come up to his questioningly that, to explain his interruption, he added : " It has begun to rain. There will be a storm, I think. Better shut the window, Richard, or we shall be flooded out."

The wind had risen ; great drops, charged with light, were sliding across the panes ; the lawn had deepened its colour ; the young birch trees were tossing their heads.

" ' " I should prefer to say," ' " Carey's voice continued, " ' " that there are some men whom God is determined to win by love. Terrors and chastisements are fit for others, but these are the select natures, or, as you have yourself termed them, the courtiers of the household of God. Believe me, God does not lay traps for any, nor is he mistaken in his estimate. If he lavishes favour upon any man, it is because he knows that that man's nature will respond to love. It is the habit of kings to assemble in their houses such men as will delight them by their conversation and companionship, *amor ac deliciae generis humani*, whose memory is fresh and sweet ages after, when they be dead. Something like this it seems to me God is wont to do, that he may win these natures for the good of mankind and for his own delight. It is true that such privilege calls for a return ; but what will ensure a return sooner than the consideration of such a favour as this ? You say you have been unworthy of such favour, and have forfeited it for ever. You cannot have forfeited it, for it was never deserved. It is the Kingly grace of God, bestowed on whom he will. If I am not mistaken in your case, God will win you, and he will win you by determined and uninterrupted acts of love." ' "

At this point Carey stopped and held the book open on her knee, her finger on the place, clearly intending to continue when she could. There was no sound but the rain-beat. Soon she went on :

" ' " It may be that in some other place God would have found for you other work ; you have failed in attaining to that place ; serve him where you are. If you fall still lower, or imagine that you fall lower, serve him still in the lowest room of all. Wherever you may find yourself—— " ' " Her eyes came up from the book.

Henry Rydal, who was standing on the hearthstone looking down at her, continued from memory :

" ' " Wherever you may find yourself, still serve him, and you will bid defiance to imaginations and powers of evil, that strive to work upon a sensitive and excited nature, and to urge it to despair. . . . God is with all, with the coarse and dull as with the refined and pure, but he draws them by different means,— those by terror, these by love." ' "

Richard said : " Do you know the book by heart ? "

" Almost — that speech of Molinos."

" Did you know it ? " Carey asked Venetia.

" I remember it now."

Carey's gaze moved from face to face. At last she said : " How much did that book mean to you and Mother ? "

It was a word she had not used before in speaking of Venetia. That Venetia had remarked it, Richard could not doubt, but she allowed it to pass, as Carey herself had done, naturally.

" It wasn't a book of the Fates, if that is what you mean," Henry replied. " It was just a book we read together on a holiday, but to find a book that stands up to happiness is rare — rarer, even, than to find a consolation when the room's empty."

At this, Venetia turned her head away. Her hand travelled to her face as if she wished to shut out what her eyes were seeing. In a moment, she recovered herself. Her gesture, her taking away of her hand, her refusal to cover her eyes, had had in it nothing of fear or shrinking and so much of decisive courage that Richard knew instantly towards what decision she was making her approach, and was glad to think, when the evening ended and she said good-night to them all and went to her room, that at any rate the decision was not yet made. The danger, as he saw it, was that she had ceased to dramatize herself. In her present mood, if it were to continue, she might have the courage of her despair.

He did not sleep. It was in his mind to go to Henry Rydal and tell him what he feared, but he hesitated. What held him back was an assurance that he must not be absent from his own room. Venetia had confided in him once. Perhaps, if she were in great stress, she would come to him again. Hearing, as he thought, a knock on his door, he called out, but none entered ; and he decided that the tapping of creeper on his window had misled him. The wind was high and, when he looked out, the dark clouds were swirling over a pale horizon.

Soon afterwards he heard unmistakably a footstep on the landing. So sure was he of his intuition that he moved towards the door, his hand stretched out to open it, but the footsteps passed and began to ascend the stair leading to the attic. He picked up a torch from beside his bed and followed.

By the time he reached the upper landing, the door of the attic had been closed, but it fitted ill and from beneath it a disk of light lay out towards him. He asked himself for what Venetia could be searching in the attic — perhaps for some memento of the past that she was resolved to take away with her. There was always in him a reluctance to force his presence on anyone, particularly on one who believed herself to be alone and secure against interruption ; but his mind was clear ; not to intervene now might leave him with everlasting regrets ; so he went forward, knocked and, receiving no answer, opened the door.

It was not Venetia he found, but Carey. The attic was large, with a roof sloping downwards to his right, almost to floor level, the only window, boarded up, being set among the rafters. It was full of wooden cases, trunks, old files, pieces of furniture, among them a railed cot that had been made a depository for a doll's house, a white ewer and a wooden figure of a dusty negro with large, painted eyes. At the farther end of the room Carey was standing beside the cot. She was in her night clothes and wore the wrap in which he had first seen her. Her candle, set down on a low packing-case, threw her cheek shadows upward, and, as she seemed not to have heard him enter and did not turn her head, her eyes were shadowed, and he did not at once follow their direction or understand at what she was intently looking. So still was she that he did not speak or move ; his words to Venetia returned to his mind and he asked himself whether Carey was sleep-walking ; but the question answered itself in the nature of her stillness ; she was awake and aware, all the late disturbance of her spirit was gone, she had that composure, that vitality in rest, which portraits may have, but seldom the human countenance, over which experience travels, for the most part, so fleet-ingly that in no single instant is the essence of character distilled.

A candle-beam on the edge of a gilt moulding hinted to Richard that she was looking at a picture set up on the floor with its back so nearly turned to him that he could not see the canvas, and though his identification of the picture followed naturally and at once, it came to him as a shock that, at this hour of night, she should have come to look at her mother's portrait and that so remarkable a beauty should have been given, or restored, to her face by the contempla-tion of it. There was, in this beauty, something rapt and breathless and, at the same time, fallible, which drew his heart towards her, and his love for her now told him how imperfect his former love had been.

When she saw him, it was with no surprise, rather with a glad and natural recognition. She moved towards him as he advanced, and came into his arms, without, seemingly, the need of decision, as though it were predestined. In answer to him, she said :

"I want only to be with you, my dear love."

The candle was behind her. Its light flowed up to her hair, but he could see, as he held her, only the shape, not the detail, of her face. Knowing that she had undergone an experience the nature of which was as yet concealed from him, he desired to see her, and turned her body under his arm so that she also faced the candlelight ; and, seeing her then and the lovely fall of the cheek that she had inherited, he remembered the portrait which she so closely resembled, from which she so profoundly differed ; and suddenly she gave the future to him ; his mind leapt out across the years ; he saw this instant, not as a present encounter between two beings separated by age and circumstance, but as part of a continuity that was their life together. Whatever words they might say now would but confirm an unspoken betrothal, and they said none but the little words of mutual acceptance and joy, until presently she asked :

"Do you remember my telling you of the night when I was small and went into Venetia's room ? Everything repeats itself. This evening, downstairs, when she gave me that book and I was reading it, I began to love her. . . . ' Began ' is wrong ; it happens suddenly. . . . It was like going out of a thick wood and feeling the sun on your face, hands, arms, your whole body, everywhere. It wasn't for her alone; she was included in it — in the warmth and light, I mean." Carey paused, struggling for words in which to communicate her experience. "You lie on the earth," she said, "and that's nothing — something to lie on — you are thinking of yourself. Then you turn over on your face and spread out your arms and you are holding all the earth and——" She broke off, smiling; then continued: "I felt how young she was and how lonely and how eager to come in, and how miserably, miserably in despair of ever being admitted. I felt it in my own blood and bones; it was I who was shut out as much as she; — and yet, when she said good-night, and looked at me *with my own eyes* as if she would never see me again, still I could do nothing and say nothing; I let her go. But in my own room," Carey went on, her phrases sharply stopped by a quickened breath, "I began to think of her again as I did when I was a child, when her room was empty but I knew she was in it, and I wasn't afraid, and it seemed natural and right that she should be in it, and I went to look, and Father came. . . . If I go to her room now," she added after a long pause, "I shall find her."

"I will wait for you. I want to see you again to-night," Richard said. "This is a precious night. My life begins with it."

They went down together to the first landing. At the door of his own room he stopped, intending to wait there until Carey should have gone into Venetia's. Up to this point he had had her own assurance of the wisdom of her going, but now was afraid of what she might find. As her hand disengaged itself from his, he drew her back and held her and whispered : " Carey, you said she looked at you as if she would never see you again. What did that mean ? "

" Perhaps that she meant not to stay with us."

The reply was doubtful. Clearly, no shadow of the fear in his own mind had fallen upon her. She was tranquil, the candle steady in her right hand.

" Go, Carey," he said. " I think there is no time to waste."

Her look was surprised, but she obeyed without question, crossed the landing and knocked at Venetia's door. Whether she received an answer he could not hear. She entered and closed the door behind her. He waited in fear, almost in expectation, that she should cry out and return, her face altered, hastening, full of alarm ; but a minute went by in silence, and he found himself in the darkness, the knob of his door under his fingers. Knowledge of his own life flowed back to him ; he was lifted by the extreme joy of it, as if he were a young man again ; it seemed to him that the private and inward happiness now given and promised was proof against the disintegration of the world, and rather than shut himself into his own room he lighted his way downstairs with his torch, eager to be in the air. As he entered the garden, the wind, that he had forgotten, struck at him, but he went on across the lawn, through the gate, his thought swerving to the work he was doing at Glazeden, which appeared to him now, not as a task limited by its special purposes, but as an incident in a life that included the war and stretched beyond it. Across a bend in the road, a cart-track, now dully illumined by the sky's leaden and intermittent glare, reached out into the fields, barred, as it entered them, by a gate. Here he found Rydal leaning.

"Couldn't sleep. Too hot and stormy. And you?"

"I came out for the air."

Rydal handed him a tobacco pouch. "Stay and smoke. Shelter your match. We don't get the Glazeden sirens when the wind is this way, but there's a raid on. Listen."

There was a throb of bombers in the air and far away to the south-west the silent flash of bursting shell.

"Not London at any rate," Richard said.

"No. They are too wise."

"Too wise?"

"And yet they may not be," Rydal continued. "They are an odd race. They have a pathetic belief in frightfulness. London will tempt them. Their business is with the airfields by day if they have the guts, and they have guts all right as long as they have the odds — but Bond Street may tempt them. Pray God! We can do without Bond Street."

The wind was falling; the sky cleared to a half-moon as they returned.

"Henry, I am going to marry Carey. May I with your good-will?"

"She has said so?"

"Not — in — so many words."

"You forgot to propose? . . . Or she to you? . . . That's as it should be. . . . When?"

"To-night. An hour ago."

"Then where is she? Why isn't she here?"

"She went to her mother's room."

"To tell her?" Rydal's tone sharpened. "Carey — to tell *her*? Why did she go?"

"Not for that reason."

"For what reason, then?" — this with a tormented, an almost angry suspicion. Then, as Richard did not at once reply, Rydal continued: "I think it's the end with us, Richard. She means to go. I knew it to-night. I can't keep her. I thought that she and I and Carey — you, too, perhaps——" He walked on in silence. "To 'start again' isn't enough," he continued. "To do myself credit, I always knew that. You have to be reborn. Perhaps nations can be because the old generation dies and a new generation is bred and grows up. Their past lies down in the grave. They lay their ghosts. Perhaps human beings can't. May be that's where I was wrong."

"Have you ever fully forgiven her, Henry, for what she did?"

"Forgiven? No. Not as a separate act. It's not necessary. You 'forgive' a stranger, not a woman you love. I have always loved her. Love includes forgiveness of every wrong before it is committed — before, after, at all times. But I have lost her," Rydal added. "Where she will go to, I don't know. I suppose, for what it may still be worth, I shall track her down."

"If she went, I don't believe that," Richard said.

"What?"

"That you'd find her again."

"In time, I should."

"Not where she was going."

Richard had expected that Henry would be sceptical of Venetia's power to kill herself, but he answered: "Carey *is* with her? She *is* safe?"

"Carey went from me to her. I should have known if she was not safe."

When they reached the lawn, Rydal halted, looking at the upper window. " What made Carey go ? You ? "

" She went of herself, Henry."

Rydal's face came round to his. " Of herself," he repeated. " Once," he said, " when she was a child, she thought there was a ghost in that room. I had to quiet her — anyhow I thought I had to ; I took her into my own bed ; we sang songs, I remember ; she asked me what it meant to *lay* a ghost. She wanted to know how to do it. I told her — God help me. What would your answer be to a child who asked you how to lay a ghost ? "

With the delight of a story-teller who, in his story, supplies a prompted answer to the insoluble riddle, Richard said : " Songs and love, Henry."

Rydal seized his arm. " Carey told you the answer ! "

" Yes."

" She remembered it ! Ah my God," Rydal exclaimed, " she remembered it ! That comes back ! "

As they reached the door a glint of light appeared at their side from the blacked-out window of the sitting-room. In the hall, Rydal called out : " Carey ! " and entered. She was seated on the music-stool, facing them. He began at once to question her, but she broke in and said :

" She is well, and happy, and asleep."

" Was she asleep when you went in ? "

" No."

" Tell me, Carey. Tell me all there is to tell. When you found her——"

" We talked, Father. Not much. I held her in my arms. Then she asked me to read to her and I did. Then she said she wanted to see you. Then quite suddenly she kissed me and was asleep."

" I will go to her," Rydal said.

Carey put her hand on his arm. " No. You have all your lives. Go to her in the morning when she wakes."

London : Spring 1941.

THE END

Printed in Great Britain by R. & R. CLARK, LIMITED, *Edinburgh.*